W9-AQO-694

AN **ALEC FLINT** MYSTERY

The RANSOM Note BLues

Also by Jill Santopolo

An Alec Flint Mystery:

The Niña, *The* Pinta, *and the Vanishing Treasure*

AN **ALEC FLINT** MYSTERY

The RANSOM Note BLues

by
Jill Santopolo

Illustrations by Nathan Hale

Orchard Books / New York
An Imprint of Scholastic Inc.

ISBN-13: 978-0-439-91255-6
ISBN-10: 0-439-91255-5

10 9 8 7 6 5 4 3 2 1   09 10 11 12 13

Printed in the U.S.A. 40
First edition, June 2009
Book design by Tim Hall

To my sisters, Ali and Suzie,
and to my grandfather, Michael V.,
who spent a summer afternoon
walking around the Pollack-Krasner House with me
instead of lounging on the beach.

Contents

1

Yelling in Ear Holes

Alec Flint, official super sleuth-in-training, sat on the kitchen floor reading the notes in his detective journal. Gina Rossi, official super sleuth-in-training partner, read over his shoulder.

"Look." Alec showed Gina one of the pages. "I should've figured out that Emily Berg's mom was going to make her get a haircut. See all the times I wrote down that Emily came onto the bus with her hair all messed up and her mom running behind her with a headband thing? Then I could've warned Emily about it. But I didn't realize her messy hair was that important."

I

"That's the thing with observing," Gina said, reaching out and flipping the pages. "Sometimes what you don't think is important ends up cracking the case."

Alec and Gina had practice at cracking cases. They solved a mystery back during the beginning of school, and it was a case that not even Alec's dad, Officer Flint, could figure out. That's why Alec and Gina got their picture in the newspaper and a whole article written about them.

But since early October, nothing very exciting had gone on in Laurel Hollows. There was the case of a misplaced toy truck belonging to one Benjamin Berg, age three, that Alec found by accident when he went searching for his soccer ball in the bushes between his house and the Bergs'. Alec hadn't even known it was missing. He didn't count it as a real mystery.

There was also the case of the missing box of

cookies at Gina's house, but Gina found out that the cookies were eaten by her father, who left the empty box in the garbage pail in his home office. She'd found the box when she was taking out the trash, which she had been studying carefully for a few days, waiting to see if the box showed up. But while Gina filed that away in her notebook as a minor case, she was looking for something bigger.

Alec and Gina were itching for a good, complicated, hard-to-crack mystery. One like the Christopher Columbus case. But instead they were stuck writing observations of things they saw in town. Alec's dad said that real sleuths wrote down everything, especially when they were on stakeouts. They never knew what would come in handy and what wouldn't. So Alec and Gina wrote everything down too.

Sometimes they even wrote it in code, so they'd get to practice. Like:

Nh. Yofnv hklpv lm z kfikov xvoo kslmv rm gsv hxsllo kziprmt olg.*

Alec's dad knew about being a real sleuth, on account of working for the Laurel Hollows Police Force, which is what Alec wanted to do when he got older. Sort of. He actually wanted to do the kind of stuff his father did, but on a bigger scale. Like for the FBI. In fact, Alec had wanted to get a job with the FBI right after the Columbus case, but Gina had informed him that you can't get a job as an FBI super sleuth if you have a bedtime of 9:17 on weeknights, like Alec did. Plus it would be good to finish elementary school first.

Gina flipped through Alec's detective book.

"Do you think maybe there's a mystery about Howard the dog?" she asked. "I mean, he does weird things like run around trees and eat snails."

*See page 163 for code translation

Alec shuddered. "No dog mysteries. I only do people mysteries."

Alec was afraid of dogs but didn't really want Gina to know that, because then maybe she'd think he was too scared to be her sleuth-in-training partner. He had good reason to be afraid of dogs, though. Once, when he was three or four and substantially shorter than the four foot six he was now, he had a very bad dog experience. A big Doberman pinscher had licked his head and face, covering him with dog breath. Alec had screamed so loudly that his uncle, in the other room, dropped a whole tray of mini egg salad sandwiches with the crusts cut off onto the floor. But thankfully that was enough to get the dog off Alec and running to eat the egg salad sandwiches. Apparently he liked no crusts a lot. The dog, that is. Alec never liked being around dogs after that. He didn't like egg salad sandwiches either. Especially with no crusts. Alec Flint was a crust sort of guy. Gina Rossi liked them too.

"Don't you think there *has* to be a mystery to solve somewhere?" she asked.

But before Alec could answer, the phone rang.

Alec popped up off the floor and grabbed it because he knew his dad was trying to take a nap in the TV room. Officer Flint had gotten up really early that morning to trail a criminal who was shoplifting Skittles from candy stores all over town. He'd caught the guy as he was heading into Stan's Candy on Broadway.

"Flint residence, Alec speaking," Alec said, the way his parents had taught him.

"Alec?" the voice on the other end said. "Is your dad there? It's Francesca. I need to talk to him. It's important."

"Gina," Alec whispered, putting his hand over the phone mouthpiece, "it's your mom."

"Does she want to talk to me?" Gina whispered back. "And why are we whispering?"

6

Alec cleared his throat.

"Not sure," he said. "About the whispering, I mean. She wants to talk to my dad."

Meanwhile, Alec and Gina could hear Gina's mom on the other end of the phone saying, "Alec? Alec? Are you still there? Alec?"

"Um, sorry. Mrs. — Francesca," Alec answered, taking his hand off the mouthpiece. He always forgot about how he wasn't supposed to call her Mrs. Rossi and was just supposed to call her Francesca, like she was his friend or something. "I'll get my dad."

Alec gave the phone to Gina and tiptoed into the TV room. He poked his dad in the shoulder. Officer Flint snored. Alec pulled on the mushy part of his dad's ear. Officer Flint rolled over. Alec was frustrated. He had practiced doing things quietly for being a super sleuth, but he had never practiced how to be loud to wake people up from sleeping.

Maybe he'd need to know this for his future jobs — like if there was a sleeping witness who needed to be questioned.

"Hey, DAD!" Alec Flint yelled into his father's ear hole. Officer Flint's eyes popped open and he reached for the empty holster on his belt.

"Cripes!" Officer Flint yelled. "What'd you do that for, Al? Is everything okay?"

"Sorry," Alec said. "You didn't wake up to poking and pulling, and Gina's mom is on the phone and she said it's important."

Officer Flint sat up, and grabbed the phone in the TV room. Alec ran back into the kitchen. Gina was sitting quietly — very sleuth-like — with her ear to the receiver. She put her finger up in front of her lips when Alec walked in. He got the message and walked over quietly, a little bit on his tiptoes, so he could hear the phone conversation too, even though he didn't really like eavesdropping.

Alec and Gina had been reprimanded, or, if you want to know the truth of the matter, yelled at a whole lot, for snooping in the last case they helped solve, but they had agreed afterward that even if it meant getting in trouble, sometimes a super sleuth got his — or her — best clues by listening in on conversations and checking out other people's stuff. They didn't do it all the time — just when things seemed mysterious. Like Gina's mom's phone call. And even then, Alec wasn't happy about it. But Gina had convinced him it was a necessary part of sleuthing. Sometimes, Alec figured, sleuthing involved doing things that made your stomach feel marshmallowy, but in the end, if it helped you to solve a case — or find a good one — maybe it was worth it.

When Alec got to Gina, he heard his dad saying, "Wait, wait, slow down, what did the note say?"

"One sec. Let me just — here it is," Gina's mom said. Then she read slowly. "'Dear Newspapermen and -women. Please print this in tomorrow's paper. I have reclaimed something from the town of Laurel Hollows that is rightfully mine. I am not asking for ransom. I will not return it. All I ask is that Laurel Hollows agrees not to press charges and lets me leave the town peacefully. Until that time, the missing object will remain hidden. I will be at the Laurel Hollows East art show Wednesday night, before the event begins. Please have an agreement there that I can sign, transferring the ownership of the hidden object. If you do not comply, I will turn your town blue.'"

Alec's dad let out a low whistle. "I'll be right over," he said. "And I'll bring the kids. I need to see that letter."

2

Listen First, Licorice Second

With their hooded sweatshirts still caught on their heads, Alec and Gina stumbled out the door after Officer Flint. Heads finally through the neck holes, the two fourth graders jumped into Officer Flint's unmarked vehicle. It was times like these that Alec was glad his mom wasn't home, because it meant there was no one else to watch him when his dad had to go be a police officer. And that meant Alec — and Gina — had to go too.

"Hey, Dad," Alec asked once he was seat-belted inside. "Are you going to put the siren on?"

Once, when Alec was in second grade, he and his

father were on the way home from the grocery store, snacking on potato chips, when Officer Flint's car intercom went off because there was a big accident right down the street. Officer Flint had pulled a red light out of the glove compartment and stuck it on top of the unmarked vehicle. He'd also turned on the siren. And because of those two things, he got to speed, which, he told Alec, only police officers and ambulance drivers can do and only in complete emergencies.

"No one's getting hurt, Al, so no siren," Officer Flint explained.

"So what's going on, sir?" Gina asked, remembering that she wasn't supposed to have heard what happened.

"Well," Officer Flint answered, "it seems that someone has taken something from the town and wants the paper to print a letter about it, otherwise he — or she — is going to turn the town blue, whatever that means."

Alec and Gina went into No-Noise Talk mode. It was something they'd been practicing since the Columbus case, when they did it for the first time without giving it an actual name. Now, since they were experts at making their mouths say words without any sound coming out, they thought it should be called something official.

Let's sleuth around when we get there, Alec no-noised to Gina.

Definitely, she no-noised back.

Then Alec saw his dad's eyes flick into the rear-view mirror.

"Are you two doing mouth stretching exercises or something?" Officer Flint asked. "Because they look like they're big enough to me."

Alec and Gina laughed. But they stopped with the no-noising. They'd have to remember not to do it when people were looking at their faces.

Once they pulled into the newspaper parking lot, Alec and Gina raced from the car ahead of Officer

Flint. Gina's mom was waiting at the door inside the reception area. She swiped a card with her face on it over a little sensor thing, and the doors unlocked.

"Mom!" Gina said. "What happened? Can we see the letter? Do you think someone's going to turn our town blue? Do you think it means blue like sad? How are they going to make us sad?"

"Now listen," Officer Flint said, coming up behind Alec and Gina. "This is official police business, so you can either watch and listen quietly, or you can go into another room and . . . umm . . ." He looked at Gina's mom.

"Hang out with the copy editors," she finished.

"And hang out with the copy editors," Officer Flint repeated. "But no questions until I'm done."

The copy editors have licorice, Gina no-noised to Alec.

Listen first, licorice second, Alec no-noised back.

So Alec and Gina listened and watched. Gina's

mom even let them have their own photocopy of the letter, since it was going to be printed in the paper soon anyway. They both huddled around their copy, and Gina wrote things down in her detective notebook:

1. No ransom — doesn't want money?
2. Look into "rightfully mine"?
3. Why at art show?
4. How make people sad?

Then Alec realized that sometimes a photocopy doesn't have all the information that the original has. So he edged closer to where Officer Flint was looking at the original and wrote in his detective notebook:

1. Person wrote note on computer.
2. Person printed note on thick, fancy-looking paper.

3. Note smells kind of sweet, like when something is baking.
4. Corner of note has some kind of blue stain — not pen.

"Did you write everything you could think of?" Alec whispered when he walked quickly and quietly to Gina.

"Yes," she whispered back. "How about licorice?"

So Alec and Gina headed over to the copy editors' office.

"Hi, Mo. Hi, Max. Hi, Rena," Gina said on her way in. "This is my friend Alec. We came to investigate the note, but now we're hoping for some licorice."

One of the men was bald. The other one looked like he had way more hair than he needed.

"Mo's being stingy today," the bald guy said. "I can't promise anything."

"I'm not being stingy," Mo answered. "I'm just mad at them," he told Alec and Gina, pointing to the other two copy editors.

"How come?" Gina asked him.

"They copyedited the whole arts and entertainment section before I got here, when they know it's my favorite part of the paper," Mo answered.

"They were the only pages ready!" Rena said.

Mo didn't respond.

"Hey," Alec said. "Maybe you could copyedit the note."

"Yeah," Gina said. "That's probably just as interesting, plus how many copy editors get to edit notes from criminals?"

Mo perked up a little bit.

"Hmmm," he said. "Not a bad idea."

Then he held out the jar of licorice to Alec and Gina. "Well, you two are welcome to have a piece anyway. It's those yahoos I'm depriving of licorice."

Max and Rena gave Mo evil looks.

Alec and Gina helped themselves and were munching on licorice when Officer Flint came to collect them and take them home. Licorice plus a brand-new complicated mystery to solve. What a perfect day.

3

Chicken Guts
and Reward Money

Officer Flint dropped Alec and Gina off at Gina's house, where her Nonna, who lived in an apartment built over the garage, was in the main kitchen slicing up chicken with Gina's little sister, Allegra. Officer Flint had asked Alec and Gina if they wanted to go to the station with him, where he had to fill out some paperwork, but they figured they should get cracking on the case as soon as possible. They even no-noised about it.

"Hey, Legs, *ciao* Nonna," Gina called as she walked into the house with Alec behind her.

"Alec and I have a new mystery. We're going to my room!"

"Maybe I'll help later," Allegra yelled as the sleuths-in-training tromped up the stairs.

Gina did not respond. She wished that Allegra would leave the sleuthing to her. It was bad enough that Allegra could already write really good poems — better than the ones Gina could write — and she was only in second grade.

"Okay," Alec said, once they'd flopped down on Gina's bedroom carpet. "I think our plan should be to solve this before my dad and the rest of the police do, just like last time."

"Deal," Gina answered, pulling out her notebook. "And maybe we'll get our picture in the paper again and another story all about it. Maybe we could even be on the front page."

"Maybe," Alec said as he pulled out his notebook too. "But we've got a lot of work to do first."

Gina took out their photocopy of the note. Alec

looked at what Gina had jotted in her notebook. Then he looked at what he'd written. He already felt like he was missing something, and Alec Flint did not like to feel that way one little bit. He ran his hands over the spikes in his hair to mush thoughts into his brain.

"Wait!" he yelled. "Gina! We didn't even realize what the biggest mystery is!"

"What do you mean?" she answered. "Isn't the biggest mystery how we get the stolen thing back before the art show?"

"No!" Alec yelled again, bouncing around the room on his green-and-black high-tops. "The biggest mystery is that we don't know what was stolen! Nobody does!"

Gina looked at him. She looked at her notebook. Then she looked at Alec Flint again.

"Oh my gosh, you're right," she said. "How are we going to get the missing thing back if we don't know what it is? And what are we supposed to do?

Walk around and ask people if they had anything stolen from them? That would take years and years and years. We'd be in seventh grade before we finished!"

"Well," Alec said, looking back at the photocopy stuck in Gina's notebook. "It's gotta be something that belongs to the whole community, I think. See this line?" And he pointed to the sentence about reclaiming something from Laurel Hollows.

"So, like . . . a traffic light or something?"

Alec Flint shrugged. "Dunno."

Gina looked back at the note.

"Wait," she said. "Did you realize this part?" She pointed to the bit about the Laurel Hollows East art show. "I mean, I realized it, but I didn't *realize* realize it until just now — we're going to be at that art show! I mean, it's *our* art show — the fourth-grade one. The one we're doing those paintings for — the ones with the dripping."

Alec groaned at the mention of the art show.

Even though Alec liked the art teacher, Ms. Blume, and felt a little bit like he had to look out for her ever since he and Gina had saved Ms. Blume from being trapped inside a mummy case, he didn't so much like this new project they were doing. The project was based on an artist named Jackson Pollock who, as far as Alec Flint could tell, mainly just dripped a lot of paint on a really huge canvas and said, "Hey, everyone, I finished a painting!"

The whole fourth grade was doing a unit on Jackson Pollock because of an old rich lady. This lady was not an anonymous benefactor — in fact, she was very *nonymous*, if that's the opposite of anonymous, which Alec Flint thought it might be. The old rich lady had given every fourth grader a canvas and paint and other things, with the rule that the school had to use them to teach students about Jackson Pollock. She also was sponsoring the party at the art show. She had a kind of interesting name, but Alec couldn't remember it. . . .

"Hey, what's that old rich lady's name again?" Alec asked. Gina was good at remembering things like names of old rich ladies.

"Penelope LaViolet," Gina answered. "And she's, like, Jackson Pollock's second or fourth cousin or something like that."

"Right." Alec remembered now. She was all into Jackson Pollock because he was related to her and she wanted the whole world to know how wonderful he was, or so she said.

"Hey," Gina said, looking at the notebook again. "Do you think someone should tell her about this criminal being there? At the art show? I mean, she's an old lady. I wouldn't want her to have a heart attack and die in the middle of the show or something."

Alec rolled his eyes. "She won't have a heart attack unless she has something wrong with her heart already."

"How do you know?" Gina asked.

"Because of my great-aunt Cecile," Alec told her. "She died of a heart attack when I was in first grade, and, umm, after that, I sort of got worried that everyone was going to die of a heart attack. So my mom told me about how people only have heart attacks when their hearts are sick to begin with."

Alec was a little embarrassed about thinking that — how everyone he knew was going to have a heart attack and die right away. He hoped Gina wasn't going to make fun of him for it.

"Hey, guys! Guys! Guys!"

It was Allegra, racing into Gina's room, holding a piece of raw chicken in her hand.

"Ew, Legs, don't drip chicken guts on my carpet!" Gina said.

"What is it?" Alec said, his words tumbling right on top of Gina's. "Are you okay? Is Nonna?" He wondered if maybe Nonna had a sick heart. . . .

"It's the mayor! He just interrupted the TV show Nonna and I were watching and showed this note that got sent to the newspaper, and he's offering a reward of one thousand dollars if anyone can figure out what was stolen!"

Alec and Gina looked at each other. A thousand dollars!

That's so much money! Alec no-noised to Gina.

We're totally going to win it! Gina no-noised back.

"Umm, guys?" Allegra said out loud. "What are you doing?"

Alec cleared his throat.

"Oh, nothing," Gina said. "Thanks for the tip. We already knew about the mystery, but not the reward."

"Cool," Allegra said. "Well, I'm going to search for missing things tomorrow with Nonna. You guys can come if you want. I bet the whole town is going to be searching."

"Thanks, Legs," Gina said, looking at Alec, "but I think that we're going to search on our own. I mean, the newspaper *did* call us super sleuths-in-training."

Alec smiled big at Gina.

We can solve this! he no-noised to her. Because he knew that they could.

4

Mission: Impossible, in a Whisper Voice

Alec Flint climbed on the school bus the next morning, already rubbing thoughts into his brain. He had a note in his pocket that said he could walk home with Gina after school. They were going to work on finding the missing whatever it was on the way home. He had to come up with the best places to look. As Alec paused in the aisle to figure out where to sit, Emily Berg bonked him with a rolled-up newspaper.

"Hey, Alec Flint?" she said. "Get a move on! You can't stand in the aisle forever or Mr. Lemon won't let the bus move and we'll never get to school!"

Sometimes Emily Berg gave Alec a headache.

Alec saw an empty seat seven rows from Mr. Lemon and slid in. Emily Berg slid in next to him. She unrolled the newspaper.

"Hey, Alec Flint?" she said. "Remember how I helped you and Gina when you solved that Christopher Columbus thing?"

Alec nodded. She had helped. Not very much, but a little.

"Well, did you see this in the newspaper? There's another mystery, and I thought maybe you and Gina would want to solve it and I could help again. What do you think, Alec Flint? There's a reward too."

She showed him a page in the newspaper.

"It's sort of got splatters of milk on it," Emily said. "Sorry. But, well, there was a spill."

"There was a spill" was something that got said at the Berg house a lot. Alec knew from experience. Once when he was there, Emily spilled a whole cup of blue Gatorade on her little brother. It stained his blond hair bluish for three days.

Alec took the milk-splattered paper. On the front page was a printed copy of the letter about the mystery thing that got stolen, and then there was a note from the mayor that basically said everything that Allegra told them was on TV yesterday.

"So, are you going to solve it? With Gina? And can I help?"

Alec rubbed some thoughts into his brain. He figured that six eyeballs were better for looking than just four. But since those added eyeballs belonged to Emily Berg . . . well, he wasn't quite sure if they were going to be all that helpful.

"Sure, Emily," he said. "But we're going to look today after school. We got a tip about the mystery early because of my dad and Gina's mom. If you want to come help, you've gotta get a note that says you can walk home with us."

32

Emily smiled happily. "No problem. I'll call my mom from the office when we get to school and she'll say it's okay and bring me a note."

"They let you make phone calls?" Alec looked at her incredulously, which mainly meant he didn't believe one single word of it.

"Well," Emily answered, "sometimes they do, for emergencies. Like if you forget all your Valentine's Day cards at home when it's Valentine's Day, or if you by accident sit on the cake your mom made for the bake sale and it gets squished and also icing gets all over your dress. But I think I can say this is an emergency even if it's really not one, and then I can come!"

This was very interesting about the phone calls. If he said it was an emergency, would the office let Alec call his mom? Even though she was away on business? In Washington, D.C.? And then he could tell her that he missed her and to make sure she got home in time for the art show. He hadn't told her about the art show yet. With Alec's luck, though, if he faked an emergency, the secretary would make him call his dad, who he got to speak to all the time anyway and who would be very upset if he got a call when it wasn't really an emergency. Oh well.

"Okay, then," Alec said to Emily. "We'll go sleuthing today after school."

He'd have to remember to tell Gina.

When the bus stopped at Laurel Hollows Elementary School East, Alec and Emily got off together and walked to Mrs. Jones's class. They put their things away in their cubbies and then sat down to start the Do Now, which Mrs. Jones had on the board every day. Gina's seat was right next to Alec's — she hadn't gotten to school yet.

Alec looked up at the board. He thought it would be cool if he could get the Do Now done before Gina got there. So he started working.

*Riddle Me This: There are 7 D in a W
and 52 W in a Y.*

Well, that one was easy. "There are seven days
in a week and fifty-two weeks in a year," Alec
wrote on his loose-leaf paper. Now it was time for
Math Madness — Alec's least favorite puzzle of the
Do Now. The board said:

Math Madness: XYY − ZZZ = YZZ

Alec figured he'd skip that one for the time being
and go back to it. He moved on to the Rebus Riot.

Rebus Riot: theREADlines

Thereadlines? That wasn't a word. How could
he solve this if it wasn't a word? Alec Flint rubbed
some thoughts into his brain. The middle part was

in capitals. *Read* — well, that was a word. And the lowercase bits on either side were words too! *The* and *lines*. And *read* was between them! *Read between the lines!* Alec got the Rebus Riot! Now back to Math Madness.

As Alec started working, Gina came jogging into the classroom. She wasn't late, but she was close.

"Mom couldn't find the car keys again," she said as she sat down and began to work.

Alec saw her write down the answers to the riddle and the rebus quicker than he had and start on Math Madness. He focused back on his own paper.

He began by making all X's and Y's 1 and 2, and Z's 0, but it didn't work because anything minus a zero is itself. So if Z were 0, the answer would be XYY, not YZZ. Then Alec tried 3's, 2's, and 1's. And it worked! He sang the *Mission: Impossible* theme song quietly, in a whisper voice, so that only Gina could hear him. It was his code to her that he'd finished the Do Now.

Gina glanced over at Alec's paper.

"There's another answer for Math Madness," she whispered.

The thing with Gina and Math Madness on the Do Now is that she always got it, and always got it with more than one answer. Really quickly. Alec sighed. One answer to Math Madness was enough for him, because his method of starting with 0 and plugging in numbers until he found the right one was very time-consuming. And a little boring.

"How do you do it so quickly?" he whispered.

"You've gotta figure out the relationships between the numbers," she whispered back.

Alec didn't quite get what she meant, and was about to ask, when Do Now time was done. Mrs. Jones went over the answers, and then told everyone it was time for a lesson on Jackson Pollock, the artist they were studying with Ms. Blume in art class. The one who did drip paintings.

"Ms. Blume is going to teach you about his

painting techniques, and I'm going to teach you about his life," she told the class.

Alec perked up. This part might be interesting. Maybe they'd even find out why people thought this dripping paint stuff was good art. Three months ago, some guys had come and painted the living room and the kitchen in Alec's house. They had drop cloths that they put down to catch the paint. That way Alec's mom wouldn't get mad that the floors got ruined if there was a spill. When the guys were done, the drop cloths looked a little bit like Jackson Pollock's paintings, with all the drips and splatters and splotches. And those weren't art, not even a little. Those were just mess.

"The first thing we're going to learn about Jackson Pollock is that he was married to another artist. Her name was Lee Krasner."

Alec wondered if maybe he would marry another FBI sleuth when he got older and was an FBI sleuth himself. It was an interesting thought, being older and sleuthier and married. He peeked at Gina and saw her peeking at him. Alec Flint looked back at his desktop very quickly. He didn't want her to get any ideas.

"Lee Krasner and Jackson Pollock were both abstract expressionists. That means that they didn't really plan out their paintings — they created things as they went along. And they painted from their emotions. So if Lee Krasner or Jackson Pollock were feeling sad one day, the paintings would come out looking sad. They didn't paint things exactly the way that they looked in real life either."

Emily Berg raised her hand.

"What does it mean that a painting would come out looking sad?" she asked.

Alec looked over at Gina to see if she knew. Sometimes if Gina knew an answer, she would tell Alec, even if really she should've raised her hand and told the whole class. Gina didn't say anything. Alec guessed she didn't know either. Or maybe she was just figuring out the best way to say the answer. That happened sometimes too.

"It's . . ." Mrs. Jones started, then stopped. "What do you think it means?" she asked Emily.

Oooh, Alec hated that teacher trick. The one where the teacher made you answer your own question. It happened to Alec once when he asked if he really had to write five whole pages about Christopher Columbus. Mrs. Jones had said, "What do you think, Alec?" And he had said, "I think I have to," very glumly. And Mrs. Jones had said, "You think right." Which was just too bad because even though knowing things about Columbus helped Alec solve a case, he still really didn't like that explorer very much.

"Does it mean they paint frown faces?" Emily answered in her question sort of way.

Gina rolled her eyes. Then she whispered to Alec, "Didn't she hear Mrs. Jones say *abstract*? When things are abstract, they don't look really like any-thing. Especially not frown faces."

Alec kept his mouth shut. He hadn't known what abstract meant either.

Gina raised her hand. Roy Michaels did too. Mrs. Jones called on Roy Michaels.

"I think," he said, "that a sad painting where things aren't painted the way they look means . . . that, for example, you'd maybe paint it blue and gray because those are sad colors. And there would be lots of drips that maybe look like crying. And also maybe part of a frown, but not a whole frown face."

"Exactly, Roy! That was wonderful," said Mrs. Jones. "Gina? Do you have anything to add?"

"Not that much," said Gina. "Only that you can set the mood of a painting with the colors you use and the shapes that you use and how much paint goes on the canvas. Like if you're feeling really crazy and busy, you'd maybe put on a lot of paint, or if you're feeling lonely, you'd put on only a little."

"Another great answer!" Mrs. Jones said. "I think we might have some artists in the room."

Alec saw Roy and Gina smile. He wished he could've given good answers like that.

"How did you know that stuff?" he whispered, real quietly, to Gina.

"I did painting club over the summer at camp," she whispered back. "They taught us lots of stuff there."

Painting club. Alec didn't even know there was such a thing. He'd never gone to summer camp. But maybe this summer he would. Maybe they had a super sleuth club. He'd always wanted to learn how to track people from tire marks and footprints. . . .

Then Mrs. Jones looked at the clock and made an announcement. It was time for a special art class that they didn't usually have on Tuesday so they could keep preparing for the art show. Two days in a row was a lot of art. Plus it meant no P.E.

"Quickly and quietly!" Mrs. Jones said, clapping her hands — which meant the whole class had to get into two double lines to travel to art.

Gina stood next to Alec.

"Hey," she whispered to him. "What kind of mood is your painting?"

Alec thought about it for a while. He didn't really know. But then it hit him.

"Annoyed," he said. "My painting is annoyed."

Gina giggled, and they both followed the line out the door.

5

Six Eyeballs Are
Better Than Four

At the end of the day, Alec showed his note that said he could go home with Gina to Mrs. Jones. It was time for them to do some sleuthing. Once their jackets and backpacks were on, Emily Berg came over, dragging her stuff on the floor behind her.

"I'm coming too, Alec Flint!" she said. "Remember you said I could come too?"

Alec didn't remember — but only for three seconds or so. Then he did remember. About the bus and the phone call from the office and Emily's mom bringing the note and all of that. And also how he forgot to tell Gina.

You said Emily could come? Gina no-noised at him, with a look that she usually reserved for when she was mad at Allegra.

Sort of, he no-noised back. *I'll explain later.* He was hoping the angry-dog-about-to-bite-someone look would get off of her face before he had to explain.

"If we find what's missing, we'll split the prize money three ways, right?" Emily said. "I want to buy a pony. Or maybe two ponies and a hamster."

Alec shuddered. Along with dogs, he didn't like hamsters. He'd never had a bad hamster experience; he just thought they were kind of creepy. He didn't answer Emily's question. Neither did Gina.

Alec, Gina, and Emily all walked out of the school together.

"Come here," Gina said, when they were a block or two away, her eyebrows still a little scrunchy. There was a bench in a little quiet garden, right next to the sidewalk, and Gina sat on it. "We need a plan."

Gina was good at plans.

"Well," Alec said, glancing at the thief's note again, "the thing that's missing belongs to the whole town. What sorts of things belong to the whole town?"

"The park!" Emily said.

Gina looked surprised. Alec wasn't that surprised. He knew that Emily had good ideas inside. It's just that sometimes they had trouble getting from her brain to her mouth.

"I think the park is a good place to start," Alec said. "We can see if any of the playground stuff is missing. That belongs to the whole town."

Gina agreed, but sort of slowly. Emily agreed much faster. So the three of them started walking. On the way, they passed other groups of people — kids and adults — who seemed to be looking for the missing something too. Everyone wanted that prize money.

Once they got to the park, Alec stopped. He had been thinking about something for the whole walk to the park.

"Listen," he said. "It's hard to figure out what's not in a place. Like, for example, if you had seven grapes, and I ate one while you weren't looking, and then you came back, would you realize?"

"Probably not," Emily said.

Gina nodded.

"Exactly," said Alec. "So what we're going to have to do is try to remember in our heads what things looked like before, and then compare them to what we see now. So then it will be like looking at a picture of seven grapes and a picture of six grapes, and just seeing what is different. That's what I did to remember things after the Columbus exhibit went missing, and it worked. Sound good?"

"Sounds good," Emily said.

Gina nodded again. "Good thinking, Alec," she said, her eyebrows unscrunching a little. "We'll do mind pictures."

So they walked through the park and kept stopping in different places to close their eyes, look at pictures in their brains, and then open their eyes to see if the pictures matched what they saw in front of their faces. Everything was looking the same until, all of a sudden, Emily jumped up and down, did a little twirl, and then tripped on a pinecone.

"I got it!" she yelped, not even upset that she fell. Alec figured she was used to it. Falling, that is.

"It's a tree! The person stole a tree!" she said. "There used to be a tree right near the slide and it's gone! I know because once I fell off the stairs where you climb up the back of the slide and hit the tree on the way down and scraped my whole arm. There's still a scar, a little bit, see?"

Alec looked at Gina. Gina rolled her eyes up to the clouds. Alec did a little cough.

"Umm," he said. "I don't think the person stole a tree. I think probably it got chopped down because kids were getting hurt on it."

"Yeah," said Gina. "Actually, I don't think it went missing recently. I think they chopped it down a few months ago. Besides, once you chop down a tree, it's dead. Unless you want to build something or make a fire, it's not really all that valuable. I don't think the town would really care if a tree went missing."

"Oh," said Emily, looking down at her sneaker toes with droopy eyes. Alec hated it when she looked like that.

"But you did a good job, Emily!" he said. "You found something that was missing. That was good, even if it's probably not what the thief stole."

The three of them kept walking.

"Look," Gina said quietly. "The water fountain is gone. And there's a workman hanging around where it used to be. Maybe he's the thief in disguise. Didn't your dad say the thief usually comes back to the scene of the crime?"

"Why would a thief want a water fountain?" Alec asked. "I mean, it's better than a tree, but still . . ."

"Maybe the thief is a really thirsty person," Emily offered.

"Maybe," Alec agreed. "I guess it's possible. . . ."

"Well," said Gina, "I'm going over to question the workman. Anyone coming?"

Was she kidding? Of course Alec was coming! Part of what super sleuths did was question possible bad guys to see if they were for-real bad guys.

"I am," he said.

"Me too," said Emily.

All three of them walked over to the workman.

"So," Gina said, trying to act like nothing was weird, "what's going on with the water fountain?"

Alec had to give her sleuth points for being direct, but he realized she'd forgotten the first thing Officer Flint had told them about interviewing witnesses or suspects — ask them their name.

"Old one's gone," the workman said.

Alec cleared his throat.

"What's your name, sir?" he asked. "And where did the old fountain go?"

"Bob," the workman said. "And the old one went to the dump. It was broken. New one's in my truck. Wanna see?"

Alec was suspicious. Why didn't the guy give them his whole name? Maybe there wasn't a new water fountain in his truck. Maybe he was bluffing.

"Sure," Alec said. "I love water fountains. It would be cool to see a new one."

Gina and Emily gave him funny looks.

Have to see if it's a bluff, Alec no-noised to Gina.

"What?" she said out loud.

Bluff, Alec no-noised again, remembering how it was easier to understand no-noising when it wasn't a whole sentence.

Got it, Gina no-noised back.

The three of them followed Bob to his truck, which was in the park, about three feet from the place the old water fountain used to be. Another workman was there, wheeling a big water fountain down a ramp.

"There it is," Bob said. "New fountain."

Clearly, these guys were not the thieves and the water fountain was not the missing something.

"Cool," Alec said, still playing the part of a boy who likes water fountains a whole lot.

"Um, I think we have to go now," Gina said to Bob. "But thanks for the info about the fountain."

"I thought we almost had it that time," Emily said as they started walking. "It seemed like it really could've been the water fountain that was stolen."

"I think," Gina said, "that we need to think about things that people would *really* want to steal. Like . . . things that are expensive."

"Like cars!" said Emily. "Cars are expensive!"

"Um," said Alec, "I think more like jewelry or art."

"The town doesn't own any jewelry all together," said Gina.

"But they do own art," Alec said. "And I know where!"

He raced down the path in the park until he got to the rose garden. There were tons of statues there — people and horses and one of a bird perched on someone's shoulder — and statues were big-time art.

"Okay," he said, "are any of the statues missing?"

They all closed their eyes and concentrated on their brain pictures of the rose garden. Then they opened their eyes.

"I don't think so," said Gina.

"Me neither," said Emily.

Alec sighed. He didn't think so either. "Well, at least it was a thought."

Emily looked at her watch. It was pink with a twirling ballerina whose legs were the time arrows.

"My mom is going to get me in ten minutes in front of my dad's office — she said wherever we sleuthed in town, I should meet her there at four-fifteen because of getting home in time for my math tutor. You guys want a ride?"

"I'm going back to Gina's," Alec said, glancing over at her, "and I think we were going to walk."

"Nah," said Gina. "We'll take the ride. I'm tired."

Plus, she no-noised to Alec, *I have an idea*.

The three fourth graders walked through the park toward the street where Emily's dad had his office. They ambled past the duck pond, where there were no ducks.

"Hey!" Emily said. "Maybe someone stole the ducks!"

"No," Gina replied. "They flew south for the winter."

"Yeah," said Alec. "Remember from science?"

Emily shrugged. "Not really, but I believe you."

They kept walking until they reached the street. Then they turned left.

"Are you sure this is the right way, Emily?" Gina asked.

"She's sure," Alec answered. "And I'm sure too. I've been there before."

Emily was busy checking the ballerina's legs.

"Hey," she said. "Are you guys sleuthing again soon? Because maybe I could help then too. I really want that hamster. And those ponies."

Gina no-noised at Alec, *No way.*

He figured that meant he was the one who was going to have to tell that to Emily. But he couldn't!

"Umm," he said instead. "We'll have to see how it goes. Okay, Emily?"

"Sure," Emily said. "Just let me know. All right?"

"All right," he answered.

In a few more minutes, they'd reached Alfred Berg's insurance agency. Emily's mom's minivan was out front, and Emily ran toward it.

"Hey, Gina," Alec whispered. "Do you think Emily should ask her dad if anyone's reported something big stolen?"

Gina looked at Alec with that mad-dog face again. He snapped his lips shut. Alec and Gina climbed into the backseat. Alec had to move some of Ben's tank engines off of his seat, and Gina picked up an apple off of hers.

"Mom, you're wearing it!" they both heard Emily squeal. Then she turned around. "Look at my mom's ring," she said.

Alec and Gina peered up toward Emily's mom's hand. There was a ring with a big red stone in it sitting on her middle finger.

"It's nice," Alec said.

"Yeah," agreed Gina.

"Why are you so excited about your mom wearing that ring?" Alec asked Emily. "I mean, other than that it's pretty."

"Oh," Emily said. "It's 'cause my grandma left it to my mom in her will when she died, and Grandma's mom left it to her, and in a very long time when I'm old and my mom's older and one day she dies, she's going to leave it to me, right, Mom?"

"Yup," Emily's mom said. "Someday far in the future, hopefully."

"So really," Emily said, "it's kind of my ring too."

"Did anyone ever leave you anything in a will?" Alec whispered to Gina.

"No," Gina whispered back.

Alec liked this concept of leaving people things in a will, even though it was kind of shivery to think about dying. Maybe he could just leave people things and be alive. Like, when he was done with them. For example, Benjamin Berg really liked

Alec's old train set. And Alec never played with it anymore. He should write an alive will that said Benny could have it.

And just as Alec decided to do that, the car stopped.

"We're here!" said Emily's mom.

"Thanks, Mrs. Berg," Alec said.

"Thanks," Gina echoed. "And your ring is really pretty."

Once the van pulled away, Gina grabbed Alec's arm and tugged him toward the house.

"What's the rush?" Alec asked, stumbling after her and feeling like Gina was going to pull his arm right out of his shoulder socket.

6

Police Car Partners
Don't Blab

"So what's the idea?" Alec said, when they got to Gina's room.

Gina paused. "Actually, before I tell you my idea. I need to talk to you about something else. It's about being good partners."

Alec got a little nervous. Things never went well when people said they needed to talk. For example, needing to talk at Alec's house usually meant his mom had to go on an extra-long business trip, and once it meant that his grandparents were moving far away. All the way to Florida. Alec sat down on Gina's bed and untied and retied his sneakers.

"Okay," he said. "What's going on?"

Gina looked a little nervous too. Or maybe just uncomfortable, like her clothes were all itching her at the same time.

"It's like this," she said, staring at the poster that hung next to her closet and had flags from a million different countries on it. "I don't mind Emily Berg. I think she's okay, mostly — but you don't have the right to invite people to sleuth with us. You just don't, Alec Flint!" She turned and looked at Alec, and her eyebrows had scrunched up even more than before.

Alec knew he should have told Gina about Emily, but he didn't expect her to get all mad like this.

"You know," he said, louder than he meant, "we wouldn't have even solved the Columbus case without her!"

"I don't care!" Gina yelled back, staring hard at Alec, her eyebrows looking like caterpillars scrunching up on her forehead. "We're partners. That means we both get a say. Not just you. How would you like it if I went and blabbed all our secrets to Mala Sharma, huh?"

"But you wouldn't *do* that, you're not even friends with her!"

"That's not the point, and you know it," Gina said. "You'd be mad if I did. And you went and blabbed stuff to Emily. That's not how partners work. And . . . that's why I stopped before I told you my idea. Because you're a blabber."

Alec knew inside that she was right, a little bit. When he'd told Emily she could sleuth with them, he'd thought it would be hard for her to get her mom's note, but even so. That wasn't really an excuse. He just sometimes felt like Emily had so much trouble with things that he didn't want to be another trouble to add to her collection — school was hard for her and her dad was always mad at her and she never got the parts she wanted in her ballet shows, so he was always especially nice to her. And besides . . .

"Oh my gosh!" Alec said. "I get it now! You're jealous of Emily Berg!"

"I am not jealous of Emily Berg, Alec Flint, I'm just jealous that —"

"Aha!" Alec said. "So you are jealous!"

"No! I just said I wasn't! Aren't you listening?"

"I am! And you just said — "

"Oh, forget it. You'd never understand. You're just a not-listening blabber who doesn't understand about partners."

But Alec Flint did understand about partners.

"Like police car partners," he finally said. "Like how if my dad and Pete didn't listen to each other or tell each other all the facts about a case, they might get hurt chasing a perp. We have to be partners like that. Right?"

"Right!" said Gina. "That's exactly what I've been trying to say!"

She looked relieved.

Alec Flint looked relieved too.

"I'm sorry," Alec said. "We'll be like police car partners from now on."

"You promise?" Gina said. "Pinky swear? And pinky swear you won't ask Emily to sleuth again without talking to me about it first?"

Alec hooked his pinky in Gina's and they both kissed their thumbs.

"Pinky swear," he said.

Alec was glad that was over.

"Okay," Gina said, sitting down on the floor and crossing her legs. "Then let's get down to business. Oh, and, um, I'm sorry I called you a not-listening blabber. I was just, you know —"

"It's okay," Alec said, being an understanding partner. "Don't worry about it."

Gina cleared her throat. "All right, then. So I thought of this idea because of your idea with the statue garden. It's not just that the thing has to be valuable and belong to the whole town, it has to be movable too — like, very easily. So we should just figure out what things like that exist. I don't think a lot will fit that bill."

"Fit that bill?" Alec asked.

"It's an expression," Gina said. "It means that something will be all of those things."

"Oh," Alec said. "Got it. So . . . what does the whole town own other than the park? That seems to be the one that is the hardest, because lots of things are valuable and movable."

"Right," said Gina. "Let's make a list. Mainly I think it's stuff that's in town buildings."

"Oh!" Alec said. "Like the pictures of different fruits in the post office?"

Alec was always curious about the fruit pictures and why they were hanging in the post office, which had nothing at all to do with fruit.

"Exactly," said Gina, "only I don't know how valuable they are. Definitely movable, though."

She wrote down the post office and fruit pictures in her detective notebook.

When they had finished their brainstorming, Alec and Gina had a list of new places to check. It looked like this:

1. Post office (check on fruit pictures)
2. City hall (what's in there anyway?)
3. Police station (small lion statue in front)
4. Fire station (Dalmatian statues on sidewalk)
5. Library (check on how valuable old books are, plus maybe they have art?)

Alec and Gina stopped after that last part. They couldn't think of anything else.

"Well," said Gina. "How do you think we should handle these places here?"

"Hmmm," Alec said. "Aren't we going on that class trip to the library tomorrow? We can ask the librarian about missing books or art then. And check out what's on the walls and stuff."

"Oh, right," Gina said, "that's perfect." She made a little note next to number 5.

"And I can ask my dad about the lion statue," Alec said. "And also about the Dalmatians. The firehouse is on his way home from work, plus his friend Bruno works there."

Gina jotted down some more notes.

"So that leaves the fruit pictures and city hall," she said.

"Well, how about we wait until we see what we find at these other places and then start on a new plan?"

Gina thought about that.

"Okay," she said. "That's fine with me, partner."

She put out her hand. Alec shook it. And just then, he heard the doorbell ring. His super-sleuth watch told him it was 6:15, which was the exact time Officer Flint said he was going to come pick Alec up.

"See you tomorrow," he said to Gina.

"Yup," she said. "And don't forget to ask your dad about the lion."

"Nope," Alec said. "Won't forget."

Then Alec remembered that Officer Flint's police car partner, Pete, was coming over for dinner that night. Maybe they'd have some top secret information on the case!

1

Losing Control of the Flings

Alec learned nothing from his dad or Pete, other than that the lion and Dalmatians were still stuck in their spots in front of the police station and the firehouse. It was a bust of a dinner, as far as Alec Flint was concerned. Meat loaf plus steamed broccoli. Alec hated meat loaf. Especially how it got cooked in a pan where you could see weird liquid bubbling up on the side when bubbly liquid was not part of the recipe. Alec always covered his with tons of ketchup and pretended it was chicken fingers and Tater Tots. When his mother was home, she reminded Officer Flint that Alec didn't like meat loaf, but when she wasn't there, meat loaf popped up for dinner. Mainly because Officer Flint said it was an easy thing to make and argued that if Alec could eat it slathered in ketchup, he couldn't hate it all that much. It wasn't like cabbage, for example, which Alec couldn't eat slathered in anything. Officer Flint never made cabbage.

Maybe it was a feeling left over from having to eat meat loaf the night before, or maybe it was that Alec remembered they were supposed to be doing drip paintings all morning again at school because the art show was that night, but Alec Flint was not happy when he woke up the next day. Even wearing his favorite green sweatshirt with the convenient pouch for storing things didn't make him feel less grumpy. Neither did adding extra gel to get his hair spikier.

So Alec grumped down the stairs, grumped his way through his Cap'n Crunch cereal, and grumped his way onto the bus, with the two dollars and two quarters Officer Flint gave him to buy the school lunch tucked away in his cargo pants pocket.

Alec plopped himself down in a window seat and grumped his seat belt on. Emily Berg plopped down and grumped her seat belt on right next to him. Her usual bounciness was gone and her eyelashes looked wet.

"What's wrong?" he asked her.

"My dad," she said, rubbing the bottom of her nose with her jacket sleeve. "He's mad because I spilled his coffee on his pants and on the floor and on a little bit of Benny. There was lots of yelling until my mom picked me up by my armpits and told me to run because the bus was here and said she'd take care of everything and I shouldn't worry. But the thing is, I'm worrying anyway. If Dad stays mad, do you think he won't come to the art show and see my painting? I really want him to see it."

Alec knew he had to be a good partner and not

ask Emily anything without checking it by Gina first, but he really wondered if Alfred Berg was in a bad mood because of having to pay big bucks to someone who got something stolen, like he almost had to do with the Columbus exhibit before Alec and Gina had solved the case. Alfred Berg would probably report something missing to the police, though, since everyone knew about this hunt for the missing something. Maybe then Officer Flint would know about it.

"Oh, I'm sure he'll come, Emily. He'll get done being upset by then."

"You think? I just wish I didn't keep doing things that make him mad," Emily said. "It's not on purpose."

"I know," said Alec, remembering the time when he and his dad were about to go to the airport to pick up his mom, and Alec had left a cupcake on the floor. Officer Flint had stepped on the cupcake in his socks and gotten very mad about the whole thing, even though it was by mistake that Alec left the cupcake there.

"You know grown-ups," Alec said. "Sometimes they get mad even when things are an accident."

"I know, Alec Flint," Emily said. "But it's still not nice."

"Yeah," said Alec. "It's not."

He'd ask his dad about Alfred Berg reporting something missing right when he got home. Time was getting short. The art show was — Alec checked his detective watch — in ten hours!

The bus jerked to a stop in front of Laurel Hollows East. Alec and Emily walked to Mrs. Jones's room together, stomping off their grumpiness as hard as they could. Grumpy stomping was something Alec's mom taught him when he was younger and sometimes it was the only thing that put him in a better mood, even though he was nine now and probably too old for grumpy stomping. When Alec and Emily got to class, Alec sat down, ready to do the Do Now. Only there wasn't one! Instead there was a note from Mrs. Jones that said: *Do Now Is Canceled This Morning. Please Spend This Time Thinking About Your Painting!*

So Alec sat and thought about how the painting was going to make him annoyed, just when he'd gotten finished being grumpy. And annoyed stomping didn't work — Alec had tried it before. But it turned out that he didn't have to worry all that much, because Ms. Blume had some interesting information to tell everyone in art class.

Once the class got there, all the kids sat on the floor next to their canvases, which were spread out from yesterday. As the students were getting settled, Alec saw Gina slip in and walk quietly over to her canvas, next to his.

Car keys? he no-noised.

Yup, she no-noised back.

Boy, Alec Flint was glad he was a bus kid.

Then Ms. Blume started talking. "Who's ready for the art show?" she asked.

"Me!" a lot of people yelled. Alec Flint was not one of those people. He was too busy remembering that right before the art show was when the thief was going to come and demand to keep the missing something, or otherwise turn the town blue. Alec was in no hurry to see his town get very sad. He'd have to find out from his dad if the police had a plan for later, in case the turning blue happened.

"Okay, guys," Ms. Blume said, opening up a big fat book with one of the drip paintings on the cover. "So, today we're going to be adding items to our paintings — putting the finishing touches on, so to speak. See, here, in this painting called *Full Fathom Five,* Jackson Pollock includes keys, buttons, twigs, and sand in his piece. He uses so much paint that the objects are covered by it completely, and it's difficult to tell what's there. So I've got a bucket of buttons, sand, twigs, leaves, acorns, and grass up here. Take whatever you like and paint it right into your piece, okay?"

Roy Michaels raised his hand.

"Yes, Roy?" Ms. Blume said.

"What about keys? Does your bucket have any of those? You said Jackson Pollock used them."

"Unfortunately, no keys here," Ms. Blume said. "But I'm sure you can find something just as good in the bucket."

"Why'd he bother to put stuff on the canvas if he was going to cover it all up anyway?" Carlos Rodriguez asked. He was standing next to Roy.

"It adds a bit of mystery, I think. See," Ms. Blume said, pointing to the book again, "in this painting you almost see the ghost of a key, but you have to look really hard to find it. You can do the same thing with these buttons or the acorns. Come check out the bucket, guys."

"I want to use keys," Alec heard Roy grumble.

Alec Flint did not want to use keys or anything in the bucket. Even if it added mystery to his painting. He liked when paintings looked like things, like people or buildings or even rubber ducks. Alec had a painting of a rubber duck in his bathroom. It was wearing a sailor hat — the duck that is, not the painting. Alec always thought it was kind of silly. But still, it looked like something.

"What's going on, Alec?" Ms. Blume came over to him. He was the only one not rummaging around in the bucket.

Alec shrugged.

Ms. Blume opened her eyes wider, like she was trying to look at his thoughts through his eyeballs. He figured he'd just tell her and save her all that eyeball work.

"Thing is," he said, "I like when art looks like things and not like drips."

Ms. Blume nodded.

"Come with me, Alec," she said. "I think you

might be one of those people who likes Jackson Pollock's earlier painting style better."

She picked another book up off her desk and flipped to a page with a big painting that looked like a Wild West scene. There were mountains and a moon and horses in it. And the horses were pulling carriages. The sky looked all swoopy, like maybe there was a storm.

"Wow," Alec said. "This is awesome."

"This is one of Jackson Pollock's early paintings, called *Going West*," Ms. Blume said. "It's one of my favorites. I love the sky."

"Me too!" said Alec.

Ms. Blume flipped through the rest of the book.

"See how his other paintings are more abstract?"

She stopped on a picture that looked sort of like a melting face made of a million different non-face colors. The painting was titled *Orange Head,* though it wasn't really orange and wasn't quite a head either.

"Huh," Alec Flint said, looking closer. "I guess this is kinda cool."

Then Ms. Blume took out another book and leafed to a page. There was a painting that looked like huge feet and legs with an eyeball in the upper right corner.

"This is kind of like *Orange Head,*" Alec said.

"Kind of," agreed Ms. Blume, "but this one was painted by Jackson Pollock's wife, Lee Krasner."

"It doesn't look as . . . as . . . angry," Alec said finally.

"What doesn't look as angry?" It was Gina, popping up behind Alec's shoulder.

He turned to her. "Lee Krasner's painting doesn't look as angry as Jackson Pollock's," Alec told Gina. "Look."

He showed her both pictures.

"Wow," Gina said, pointing to the Lee Krasner painting of the legs and the eyeball. "I love the way it looks like things are moving. And the black outline. It doesn't look angry at all. . . . It looks . . . strong, but also, maybe overwhelmed?"

Alec nodded. "Yeah, maybe, like, confused."

"What's it called?" Gina asked.

Alec looked. This book didn't have little identifiers under the artwork like the other one did.

"*The Prophecy,*" Ms. Blume told them both. "This is one of her most famous pieces."

"Wow," Gina said again.

"Okay, kids," Ms. Blume said. "You've got paintings to finish! Back to work!"

Alec and Gina went back to work.

Gina got some purple paint, and Alec finally went over to the bucket. He decided he wanted one big round button to put in the middle of his painting. And then he'd cover it with green splatters until it was the ghost of a big round button.

He picked out a handful of buttons. One was too square, another was too small, a third had what looked like a sculpture of a flower on it. No way.

He grabbed more buttons. None of them seemed right. He sat down on the floor and pulled the bucket into his lap, digging through the acorns and leaves and pinecones, until he uncovered the perfect button. Big and round and black. The best super-sleuth color around.

As he was walking back to his painting with his button, a string of orange splatter landed on his arm.

"Hey!" he said. "Watch it!"

Carlos shrugged. "Sorry, man, I guess I splattered a little too hard."

Alec grabbed a paper towel and wiped the paint until it turned into an orange smear. Good thing he'd taken off his sweatshirt before art! Paint came off of arms much easier than it came off of sweatshirts.

Whap!

Alec saw a splatter of blue paint go flying off Roy Michaels's brush and land directly on Carlos's painting.

"Dude!" Carlos said. "You're messing it up!"

"Sorry!" Roy said. "Not on purpose!"

Then a yellow splatter hit Roy's cheek. He clapped his hand to his face.

"Hey!" he said. "Who did that?"

"I didn't mean it!" L. J. said, from three people away. "It's just hard to make these flings go where you want them to!"

"Guys, guys, guys!" Ms. Blume said, panicky. "Not flings! Drips! Drip the paint, don't make it fly!"

Alec made it back to his painting without any more trouble. He dripped lots of green paint onto his button, so it got all ghosted and hidden in the painting background of gray, white, black, and green splatters. And as he was dripping, he thought of something. What if the missing something was exactly where it was supposed to be, only hidden? Just like his button, no one could tell it was there unless they looked really closely. And if you didn't know to look closely, why, you'd never see it!

8

The Nonymous Benefactor Arrives

As Mrs. Jones's class was cleaning up their paintings and wiping splatters off the floor, a tall woman with silver hair curling around her shoulders breezed into the room. She wore drapey clothes and a big silver ring with a blue stone inside it that was about six times huger than the one Emily's mom had. She floated right by Alec with her clothes fluttering behind her and left the air around him smelling sweet and sugary. It was a familiar smell, but he couldn't figure out exactly what it was. Maybe cookies? Or birthday cake?

"Hello, darling!" the tall woman said when she

reached Ms. Blume. "I was in the neighborhood and figured I'd pop by to see how everything was going. I assume this is the fourth grade? Their paintings look wonderful! I can't wait for this evening's art show!"

"I'm glad you think so," Ms. Blume said quietly to the lady. "You know, the principal keeps trying to cancel it, but the police won't let him. They said they're sure they'll have everything taken care of before the kids and their parents get there. I sure hope so. . . ." Then she turned to the whole class and made her voice louder. "Everyone, this is Mrs. LaViolet. She's Jackson Pollock's third cousin and the one who made this art show possible."

Mala Sharma started clapping. The rest of the class joined in. Mrs. LaViolet did a slight curtsy.

"Now," she said to the class, "you wouldn't mind if I looked at your paintings, would you?"

Alec shook his head no, he wouldn't mind. He saw other people shaking their heads no too. A few people, Emily included, were nodding their heads yes. But Alec was pretty sure it was because they didn't quite understand how to answer Mrs. LaViolet's question. It was a little bit of a confusing one, the way she asked it.

Mrs. LaViolet wandered around the room saying things like, "Nice color choice!" or "What an interesting decision!" or "Well, would you look at that!"

When she got to Gina's painting, she patted Gina on the shoulder and said, "Nice work, dear."

"Thank you," Alec heard Gina answer, and he glanced over to see her looking all the way up, up, up at Mrs. LaViolet. "How tall are you?" Gina asked. And then covered her mouth with her hand. "Oh, I shouldn't have asked that," she said. "That wasn't polite. I'm sorry."

Mrs. LaViolet laughed. "Oh, nothing to be sorry about, dear," she said. "I get that all the time. I'm six feet, two inches tall, on the nose."

"Wow," Emily said. "Does that mean that you're a model? My mom says that people who are really tall can be models."

Mrs. LaViolet laughed again. "How funny! No, I'm not a model. I'm a painter. Not as talented as my cousin, of course, or as Lee — but no one is. I collect them both, you know. I have some of Lee's most famous paintings in my collection."

"Do you do drip paintings?" Gina asked.

"Oh, no, dear," said Mrs. LaViolet. "I do monochromatic art."

"Does that mean everything in your paintings is the same color?" Gina asked.

"Why, yes! You're not just good at art, you're good at language arts too, I see. What a vocabulary."

Gina smiled a little bit wider.

"So what color are you painting with now?" Gina asked.

"Blue," said Mrs. LaViolet. "I'm going through a blue period."

Then she looked at her watch. "Oh! I must run! I have an appointment in ten minutes. But lovely to meet so many budding artists. I'll see you tonight! I'm sure it will be an evening written about in the papers. I can assure you, no one in Laurel Hollows will forget tonight."

Alec Flint wondered what she meant by that. Was the thief why she thought it would be written about in the papers? Or was it that she thought the art was going to be so great that the newspaper would do a story on it . . . ?

Once Mrs. LaViolet left, the class finished cleaning up and Mrs. Jones, who had appeared sometime during Mrs. LaViolet's visit, led them back upstairs to the classroom.

"She was nice," Gina whispered to Alec from right behind him in line. "And sooo tall!"

Alec nodded. "I never saw a taller girl in my life," he said. "What do you think she meant when she said the art show would be written about in the papers?"

"Maybe that it'll be really good," Gina answered.

"Yeah," Alec said. "That's what I thought." He turned back around and then immediately twisted back toward Gina. "Except . . . wouldn't she maybe be worried?"

"Yeah. I'd be worried if it was my art show. I mean, there's maybe gonna be a thief there, before the show starts. And did you hear how Ms. Blume said the principal wanted to cancel it, but the police wouldn't let him?"

"Yeah . . . so why isn't she worried?"

Gina accidentally stepped on the back of Alec's shoe. "Sorry," she whispered. "Maybe she isn't worried because she thinks the police officers are going to find the perp and it's gonna be fine."

"Yeah, I guess," Alec said, and faced forward again.

Gina poked his shoulder.

"Hey," she whispered. "Did you find anything out last night? About the case?"

"Only that the lion and Dalmatian statues are still where they're supposed to be."

Gina blew air out of her mouth in a loud breath.

"Well," she said. "The trip to the library is this afternoon, so we can see about that. If there's nothing stolen there, we'll have to check out the fruit pictures and city hall."

"Yeah," Alec said, secretly hoping that it was the fruit pictures that were missing. Then maybe the post office could put up new ones of airplanes or trucks or boats. Alec never understood what fruit had to do with delivering mail anyway. When his mom was on a business trip in Spain, she once sent Alec a package that got to him the very next day because it was sent on an airplane. At the time, Alec had wished his mom was on the airplane too.

Hmm, Alec wondered if maybe he should call the airport and alert them to the possibility of a thief making a getaway by plane after the art show with the missing something. On second thought, that didn't seem like it was enough information to go on. If the missing something was small, for example, a person could just put it in a pocketbook or a briefcase and the airport security folks wouldn't know it didn't belong to the thief in the first place.

It was also possible that the thief wouldn't travel by plane. Maybe it would be a truck or a car. Or . . . what if the stolen thing had already been swept away to another place? What if the art show was just a red herring — those fake-outs that Officer Flint said criminals sometimes did to get the police on the wrong track — and the thief was going to do something crazy to keep the police distracted tonight? Maybe the thief would set off sprinklers or throw paint all over everyone or . . . or . . .

something else crazy that would keep all the Laurel Hollows folks concentrating on the art show, and meanwhile, the thief would be getting away with the missing something forever!

Wait a minute, Mrs. LaViolet had said the art show would be something no one in Laurel Hollows would ever forget. Did she know something that Alec didn't?

Nah, that wasn't possible. Anonymous benefactors could be thieves — Alec knew that from the Columbus case — but not nonymous ones. Or could they?

Could they?

Alec Flint wasn't so sure.

9

The Speed of Peanut Butter

After lunch, which to Alec Flint's great pleasure was macaroni and cheese with peas in cheese and a cinnamon crumble cake for dessert, it was time for Mrs. Jones's class trip to the public library. They had been to the school library many times — in fact, every Wednesday from 1:30 to 2:15 — but this Wednesday, they were going on a special field trip to the big library downtown because, according to Mrs. Jones, there was something there she wanted them to see. A surprise.

The librarian from school, Ms. Klein, was going with them, as was the man who was in charge of reshelving all the books in the library on Tuesdays and Thursdays. That man, who told everyone to call him Mr. Grandpa, was someone's for-real grandpa and used to be a librarian in a huge library in New York City where they had the real stuffed bear of Winnie-the-Pooh. When he retired to Laurel Hollows, he missed the kids and the books, Mr. Grandpa, that is, not Winnie-the-Pooh, and so came to work at school two days a week. Alec liked him a lot.

Once, Mr. Grandpa saved a book for Alec — it was called *The Bobbsey Twins' Mystery at School* — and gave it to him right after the article about the Columbus case was in the newspaper. Mr. Grandpa said he thought Alec would like it, because the characters were detectives, just like Alec. Alec had liked it, and then read six more Bobbsey Twins books besides.

After everyone had put on their sweatshirts or jackets, Mrs. Jones had them line up in two single-file lines, one next to the other. Then she divided it up so that each grown-up was in charge of six kids. Alec and Gina, who were standing next to each other, and Roy and Carlos, who were standing behind them, were in Mr. Grandpa's group along with Mala and a girl named Lynnie Abrams, whom Alec didn't know very well but who had very long, very curly, very blond hair.

"So, kids," Mr. Grandpa said, "you ready for your trip to the library? Have you all been there before?"

They all nodded.

"I did the summer reading challenge," Mala told Mr. Grandpa.

"Me too," Lynnie said.

"Me too," Roy Michaels echoed. "And I got all the stickers filled on my card. I read fifty books. Got ten pencils, three erasers, and a notebook for prizes."

"Wow," Lynnie said. "I only read thirty. Just ten pencils and one eraser."

"That's pretty good," Mr. Grandpa said. "How about you, Alec, how're those mysteries going?"

"Good," Alec said. "I read a whole bunch of Bobbsey Twins, besides the one you gave me. Now I'm reading one about a girl named Ingrid for SSR — it's called *Down the Rabbit Hole* — and another one called *Whales on Stilts!* for before bed."

"Nice!" Mr. Grandpa said. "It's good to have books for different times and places."

While the rest of the group kept talking about books as they walked to the library, Alec and Gina made plans for their investigation.

"Okay," Gina said to Alec. "The plan is, we have to see Mrs. Jones's special whatever it is really quickly, and then we have to look for things that could be missing."

"Right," Alec said. "Like if there's a space on the wall that's darker than the other paint around it, that means maybe a picture was hanging there and is stolen now."

"Exactly," said Gina. "Or if there's a pedestal where it looks like maybe there was a fancy vase, but now it's missing. Especially if there's dust on top of the pedestal in the shape of something."

"Okay, good plan. And also, we can ask about expensive books that might be there," Alec said.

"Right, we can ask Louise Eleanor Allen. She's in charge, I think, and she's the one who was really nice about helping us find the Christopher Columbus stuff."

Alec liked Mrs. Allen. "Definitely. I can be in charge of asking her, if you want."

"Sure," said Gina. "That's cool."

Alec Flint whipped out his detective notebook and his pen that writes upside down and got prepared for the library sleuthing. But it looked like the sleuthing would have to wait. Once they got to the library, there was a bit of confusion. Louise Eleanor Allen was out on maternity leave because she had twin babies earlier than she was supposed to. Which would've been okay, except that the helper librarian, whose name Alec didn't know, was home sick with a really bad flu. So instead, there was a substitute librarian named Mrs. Sherwood, who had come over from another library two towns away to help out. She'd gotten to Laurel Hollows Public Library that morning.

"Hello! Welcome, everyone!" Mrs. Sherwood said, after introducing herself and explaining that she was just filling in. "I haven't looked at it yet, but I hear the surprise for you is in the lower level of the library, with the art history books. Shall we head down there?"

Mrs. Jones clapped her hands.

"Listen up, class," she said. "We have two things to do today in the library. The first is looking at the special treat in the art gallery, and the second is picking out a book for a report. Now, I know you could just as easily pick out a book in the school library, but I figured that this way you'll have some practice using the public library, and you can sign up for your own library card if you don't have one already. Sound good?"

"I already have a library card," Carlos called out.

"Well, that's great!" said Mrs. Jones. "Then you must know your way around here. You can help out anyone who's having trouble."

The other kids kept their mouths closed after that.

"Okay, since there are no more questions, let's line up and head downstairs."

Everyone lined up. Alec and Gina lined up the slowest so they could stand in the back. While they were waiting to get going, Gina saw a copy of *Little Women*.

"Hold my spot," she whispered to Alec, and quickly pulled the book out of the shelf and stuck it on a different shelf.

When she got back in line she whispered to Alec, "Now I know where it is and no one else will. I really want to do that one for the book report, but there's only one copy on the shelf."

Alec Flint thought this was a very smart thing to do. He also thought it was smart that Gina figured out which book she wanted to do her report on before they had to pick them out. He didn't know yet.

When the class finished marching down the stairs, they walked into a big room with tons of paintings on the walls and big thick books about artists on the shelves.

"Jackpot," Alec Flint whispered to Gina.

"Yeah," Gina said, sweeping her eyes around the room. "But nothing seems missing. . . ."

"Here is your surprise, kids," Mrs. Sherwood said. "A Jackson Pollock painting!" She turned and looked at the artwork. "Looks like it was from a point in his career either before or after those drip paintings."

Everyone oohed and aahed. Some people pushed forward for a closer look. Alec and Gina hung back until everyone else checked out the painting and then walked forward themselves. Roy Michaels was there inspecting it.

"Hey, guys," he said. "This painting is pretty cool. It looks . . . disturbed or confused or something."

Alec and Gina examined the painting too.

"It looks really familiar," Gina said.

"Yeah," Alec agreed. "I was just thinking the same thing. Maybe it's one of the ones we saw in Ms. Blume's book."

"What's it called?" Gina asked Roy Michaels.

"I don't know," he answered. "But I'd call it *Crazy Legs.*"

Alec laughed. "I'd call it *Walking Off the Page.*"

"You guys are so not helpful," Gina said, rolling her eyes.

She walked over to the placard next to the painting. "It's called *Full Fathom Five,*" she announced.

Something about that painting name made brain

bells go off in Alec's head, but he couldn't figure out what they meant.

All three fourth graders stared at the painting a bit more.

"He really was good," Roy Michaels said. "This painting is pretty cool. Especially that scratchy eyeball in the corner."

The eyeball in the corner, the legs . . . Alec knew there was something he was supposed to be remembering about those things, but he couldn't figure out what it was. His brain was moving at the speed of peanut butter.

"Well," Gina said after they'd looked at the painting a little longer. "I guess we should go pick out our books. . . ."

"Let's make one more circle around," Alec said. Then he remembered Roy Michaels standing there. "You know, to look at the other art."

The three fourth graders started walking around the room. Alec concentrated on the walls, making sure there were no dark spots. There weren't. At least, none that he could find. Gina didn't seem to find anything either. Roy Michaels, though, found a painting of melting clocks he really liked. He made everyone stop to admire it.

When they were done admiring, they all tromped upstairs. Gina grabbed her copy of *Little Women* from exactly where she'd left it, right next to *Mr. Popper's Penguins.*

"See," she whispered to Alec. "The best place to hide something is with other things that look enough like it that it blends right in. Then it takes a really long time to figure out where it is, if you don't know where to look."

Alec saw the truth to this. It was like the thing with eating someone's grape, only you'd have to involve a whole bowl of fruit. If you had a big pile of oranges and apples and pears and bananas, and someone added another orange, would you know? Most likely not.

"So what book are you going to do?" Gina asked Alec.

He had been thinking about this for the last ten minutes.

"I think," he said, "I'm going to do one about Jackson Pollock. I really liked that stormy sky he painted."

Alec went to the children's nonfiction section to find a Jackson Pollock book. On his way, he heard Mrs. Sherwood talking to Mr. Grandpa.

"Oh, it would be wonderful if you could help out here for a while," she was saying. "I've been trying to hold down the fort and I'm totally lost! I have no idea what happened the few days before I got here. Apparently, there were some volunteers running the place, which I guess is all that could be organized in such a pinch, but who knows what was going on while they were in charge?"

Alec wondered if people bothered checking out books when the volunteers were there. Did the volunteers even know how to use that beepy thing that made it official you were taking the book home with you? If the missing something was stolen from the library, that would've been the perfect time to steal it.

Alec had to tell Gina!

He saw her dark-haired head all the way across the library. It looked like she was jiggling the knob on a closed door, trying to open it. He walked over to her quickly.

"Hey," he said. "What's going on?"

"Look," she said, pointing to a sign. "That says this is the rare books room. There is all this stuff on the sign about how you need special permission to go in, plus you can only bring pencils into the room, no pens or crayons or markers, and no big bags or food either, and there are special hours too."

"So this must be where they keep the most valuable books!"

"Yeah, that's what I think. Only the door is locked."

"Maybe Mr. Grandpa can give us permission. He was just talking to the substitute librarian about working here for a little bit while everyone else is gone. And ready for this? There were volunteers running the library during the time that the missing something went missing!"

"For real?" Gina asked.

"Yup," said Alec. "So maybe it's one of these expensive books that's the missing something after all."

"Let's ask Mr. Grandpa."

But before they had a chance, it was time to go.

"Quick, Gina," Alec said. "Check what time the library closes. We'll have to come back later."

"Six o'clock!" Gina read off the sign on the way out. "How are we going to get back here and have time to solve everything before the art show?"

Alec checked his detective watch. Four hours and

thirty-six minutes until the art show. Four hours and six minutes until the library closed. He'd have to do some fast thinking. But he was pretty sure his peanut butter brain could handle it. At least, he hoped so.

10

Layers and Layers of Drips

Mr. Grandpa stayed behind to help out Mrs. Sherwood and get the library back in order, so Gina and Alec got put in Mrs. Jones's group on the walk back to class. She made a No Talking — Only Walking rule, so the two sleuths-in-training weren't even able to no-noise!

Back at school, they had exactly thirty minutes left of the school day. Mrs. Jones turned those thirty minutes into SSR. Alec read *Down the Rabbit Hole* quietly in his seat. It was very hard being silent because there were only — Alec checked his watch — four hours and one minute left until the art show!

Even though Alec was *kind of* following the SSR rules, he was also secretly writing a note to Gina on a piece of paper he snuck onto his lap. He and Gina hadn't been writing in code quite as much recently, preferring No-Noise Talking mode, but no-noising didn't work during SSR. Even though it was silent, your mouth had to move, and moving mouths weren't allowed. So instead, Alec jotted down the key to the code:

A B C D E F G H I J K L M N O P Q R S T U V W X Y Z
Z Y X W V U T S R Q P O N M L K J I H G F E D C B A

Then he wrote:

Trmz,
R wlm'g szev z mlgv gl xlnv slnv drgs blf.
Blf szev gl tvg blfi nln gl wirev blf gl nb
slfhv zugvi gsv yfh wilkh nv luu. Dv szev
gl tl levi lfi xofvh uli gsv xzhv yvuliv gsv
zig hsld. Rg'h lfi ozhg xszmxv gl urtfiv

lfg dszg 'h hglovm yvuliv gsv gsrvu
hsldh fk.
    — Zovx*

Alec passed the note to Gina sneakily, from his lap to hers. Then he read some of his book, until he felt a poking on his leg. Gina had written a new note. He slid it over onto his lap, trying really hard not to make any crinkly noises. It said:

Zovx,
Lpzb. Ml Kilyovn. Blfi eze droo yv gsviv, irtsg? Dv nrtsg mvvw srm.
    — Trmz*

Alec just wrote back one word:

Bvh.*

*See pages 163–164 for code translation

Ever since there was a discussion at Alec's house with his mom and his dad together about how much Mrs. McGrady's house smelled like old cat and coffee and lemon-scented air freshener, and how she never let Alec play outside and always made him sit with her in the living room while she knitted sweaters for her grandpets, Officer Flint had worked out his schedule so he could mostly be home after school. And when he wasn't, he arranged for Alec to have a playdate. But today was a home day.

As Alec was walking to the bus lines with the rest of the bus kids, he saw Ms. Blume struggling with a huge package. He stepped out of line.

"Do you need any help?" he asked her.

She peered over the top of the package.

"Oh, hi, Alec," she said. "I think I'm okay. Someone dropped off this painting in the office with a note. Said it was for the art show tonight. It's big, but it's not too heavy. I've got it."

"Did another kid paint it?" Alec asked her, wondering who would do extra work if they didn't have to. Especially on such a big canvas.

"Looks like it's from a grown-up," Ms. Blume answered, checking the note stuck on the side of the package. "Someone in the community who wanted to participate in the show. A Jackson Pollock fan, it says."

"Cool," Alec said. "It's like a mystery who the fan is."

"I guess so," Ms. Blume said. "Maybe we'll find out who it is later. Do you want to see how I've set up the art show?"

Alec looked at his super-sleuth watch. He had about seven minutes until his bus would leave.

"Sure," he said.

Ms. Blume led him to the auditorium, which she'd set up with easels. There was a plaque attached to the leg of each easel with the artist's name on it, written in Ms. Blume's loopy handwriting. Alec found the easel with his name and saw his button with the green drips in the center of his painting. He turned in a circle and saw paintings lining the wall, done by all the fourth graders — Mrs. Jones's class, Miss Goldberg's class, Ms. Werner's class, and Mr. Chu's class. He hadn't realized how many fourth graders there were.

"The room looks great," he said.

"I think so," Ms. Blume answered. "I'm going to put this one up on an easel too."

"Do you need help?" Alec asked her again.

"Nah, I'm okay. I'll see you later, though. Six-thirty sharp."

"Yup," Alec said, hoping that his mom's plane would come in on time and she'd make it to the show. Officer Flint had assured Alec that his mom knew and was planning on being there. "Okay, bye, then."

"Bye, Alec," Ms. Blume said, unwrapping the painting.

But Alec didn't actually leave. He hung around in the doorway, because he wanted to see what the grown-up Jackson Pollock fan had painted. Ms. Blume ripped off the brown paper, and Alec saw a corner of the canvas — it was covered in paint. Lots and lots more drips than Alec and his friends had done on their paintings. Ms. Blume finished unwrapping and Alec saw the rest. It looked like there were layers and layers and layers of paint. Like the person let each round dry and kept painting over it for days. Maybe even longer. If there were buttons in there, Alec would have to get really close to tell. He figured he'd check it out later.

In the meantime, he had to get home to sleuth with Gina! He ran to his bus, climbed up the steps, and sat down in the only seat left, the one right behind Mr. Lemon. It was fine, though; Alec wasn't interested in fooling around. He had to get his brain to start working much faster. Back during the Columbus case, Alec had learned that sometimes the police aren't the best at solving things. What would happen if they didn't solve this case? Would the art show be dangerous? That seemed to be what the principal thought, but not the police or Ms. Blume. Would the thief really turn the town blue? And what did that even mean? Gina had been pretty certain it meant the town would be really sad about something, but what would everyone in the whole town be sad about at the same time? Alec wished the note to the newspaper were a little more specific. He hoped the thief wasn't going to do anything that involved explosions or people getting hurt.

But then Alec made himself stop imagining different ways the thief could make people sad. All he thought about was case solving. And how he and Gina had to do it. Just in case the police couldn't figure things out. Saving the town of Laurel Hollows would be up to the two of them.

And even though that was a lot of responsibility for two fourth graders, Alec was pretty sure they could handle it.

In fact, he knew they could. They just had to get moving.

11

A Sports Car Brain

Hey, Dad!" Alec yelled on his way into the house. "Gina's coming over! I hope it's okay!"

Officer Flint appeared in the doorway of the TV room.

"That's fine, Al," he said. "I'm going to be working in here for most of the afternoon — the sergeant thinks he might have a lead on the case. They have us all doing research."

Alec's stomach swooped down into his shoes.

"Did he find out what was stolen?" he asked.

"Well, not quite, but it seems like he's found cans and cans of blue paint hidden behind city hall. I know it sounds a little ridiculous, but he thinks that might be the turn-the-town-blue threat. Not sad blue, but actual blue. And it follows then that the thief might work in city hall and probably has stolen something inside."

"Oh," Alec said. Then he wondered about the principal again, and how he thought the art show might be dangerous if the police didn't catch the perp first. "Dad? How come the police told the principal not to cancel the show?"

"Well," said Officer Flint, "if we can't catch the thief this afternoon, we'll be able to set a trap right before the show and have this taken care of before anyone gets there."

Then he heard a knock at the screen door. He turned and saw Gina through the screen.

"Okay, Al," Officer Flint said. "You and Gina keep yourselves busy, and if her mom wants, I can take you both to the art show tonight."

"Okay," Alec said.

"Oh, and Al, I spoke to Mom an hour ago. She said her meeting ran long and she's going to race to the airport, but she's not sure if she'll make her flight. She'll be home before bed, though, either way."

Alec was double bummed. Not only did the police think the missing something was in city hall, his mom might not even make it to see the art show when everyone else's mom would be there.

"Alec!" he heard Gina shout through the screen. "I see you! Come open the door!"

So he went and opened the door.

"Are you ready to continue our investigation?" Gina said once she was inside.

"The police think they have a lead," Alec informed her glumly. "And it has to do with a worker at city hall."

Gina chewed on the inside of her cheek for a few seconds.

"Did they find what was missing? Or the thief?"

Alec shook his head no.

"Well, then I think we should keep going. Come on, let's go to your room."

As the two sleuths walked down the hallway to the stairs, they heard Officer Flint's cell phone ring.

"Not what you thought?" they heard him say when he picked up. "Nothing's missing?"

Alec put his hand on Gina's arm and no-noised *Shhh* to her.

They stopped and listened. Even though eavesdropping wasn't Alec's favorite thing to do.

"Okay, I'll make the calls, just in case. . . . The park? . . . Oh, the rose garden . . . Good idea . . . Keep me posted. . . . Right . . . My kid's painting is in the art show. . . . Of course I'll be there. . . . In uniform? Sure . . . Okay, I'll get started on the calls. . . . Talk to you soon."

Alec pulled Gina's arm and the two of them raced upstairs.

"So they don't know!" Gina said breathlessly, once they got there.

"I guess not. And we already checked the rose garden! They're not going to solve this in time without our help."

Alec skipped the part where he was going to ask his dad about Alfred Berg and the insurance claims, and also the part where he was going to ask what the perp-trapping plan was if no one figured out the case by then. Those questions could wait until later. Right now, he and Gina had some fast sleuthing to do.

"Okay," Gina said, once she sat down on Alec's floor. "Let's make a list of our leads."

She pulled out her detective notebook and pen.

"Well," Alec said. "The first thing is the library. The thing was stolen the same days the volunteers were running the library, so we have to find out if any of the expensive books were stolen."

Gina wrote some notes down.

"Let's call," she said when she was finished.

"Good idea," said Alec.

He picked up the green phone next to his bed.

"Do you know the number for the library?" Alec asked Gina.

"What do I look like?" she answered. "A telephone book? Just call information — it's 4-1-1."

"I know what the information number is!" Alec said, dialing it. "I just thought maybe you knew the library number."

Alec got the library number from the person at information and called. Mr. Grandpa answered the phone. Alec recognized him from the way he said "yellow" instead of "hello" when he picked up. He did that in the school library when kids walked in too.

"Mr. Grandpa?" Alec said. "This is Alec Flint. Hi."

"Hi, Alec," Mr. Grandpa answered. "What can I do for you?"

"Well," Alec said, cutting to the chase, "do you know if there are any books missing from the rare books room? Gina's here with me and we thought maybe that was a thing the thief from the newspaper could've stolen."

"What did you tell him that for?" Gina whispered. "Now he might take our idea!"

"No, he won't," Alec whispered back, covering the mouthpiece of the phone. "He's Mr. Grandpa. He gave me Bobbsey Twins books. He won't steal our idea."

Then he took his hand off the mouthpiece.

"What did you say, Mr. Grandpa?" he asked. "I missed that."

"I was saying," Mr. Grandpa said, "that the first thing I did after you kids left today was check the rare books room. I was afraid that something terrible might have happened while the volunteers were running the place, but all the rare books look like they're exactly where they're supposed to be. Thank goodness for that!"

"Oh," said Alec. "Yup. Thank goodness for that. Well, bye, Mr. Grandpa. Thanks."

"Can I help you with anything else?" Mr. Grandpa asked.

"No, thanks," said Alec. "That's all I needed to know."

"Okay, then. You have a good night," Mr. Grandpa said.

"You too," Alec answered before hanging up.

"Well, that was a dead end," Gina said, making another mark in her detective book.

"It is about the rare books," Alec said. "But it's still possible that something weird happened at the library while the volunteers were there."

"Wait a minute," said Gina. "Do you think that

maybe the helper librarian isn't really home with a bad flu? Do you think maybe she's the thief and she ran away with something valuable after Mrs. Allen went on maternity leave?"

"Maybe," said Alec. "But if she ran off, I bet someone would've reported her missing, like they did with Ms. Blume, you know? It's been days since the missing something disappeared."

Gina sighed. "Yeah, you're right."

Both sleuths-in-training were quiet for a minute. Alec tried rubbing some thoughts into his brain. He rubbed forward and backward. Then he rubbed side to side — and it worked! He got an idea!

"Look," he said to Gina, "I think you're on to something. We've been spending all this time trying to figure out what was stolen. But let's think more like you were doing with the helper librarian and see if we can figure out *who* stole it. Then maybe the stolen thing will just pop into our brains."

"I like it!" said Gina. "Time for a new list — let's go."

She turned to a new page in her detective notebook.

"Okay," Alec said, looking at his own notes. "First thing is that the person has a computer."

"A lot of people have computers," Gina said.

"Just write it down! You never know what's important!" he said.

Gina wrote it down.

"Second thing is the person has fancy paper."

Gina gave Alec a look, but wrote that down too.

"Third thing," Alec said, "is the person either works in a bakery or makes cookies or typed this letter near something that smells sweet."

"What do you mean?" said Gina.

"The original note smelled like baking cookies," he said. "So I was using that to guess about the bakery or cookies."

"Oh," said Gina. "Well, it doesn't have to be

actual cookies that made it smell that way. It could be from perfume. Or cologne."

Alec thought about that. It definitely could be. Not necessarily, but it could.

"Okay," he said. "Write that down too."

Gina did.

"Fourth is the person wrote the note near something blue that rubs off, like paint or markers."

Gina wrote that too. Then she looked up at Alec.

"That's all I got," he said.

Gina tore the page that she had just been writing on out of her notebook and gave it to Alec along with her pen. Then she flipped back to her list.

"My turn," she said. Then she read from her notebook. "The person doesn't want ransom money, so that means he or she isn't poor."

"And if you count in the fancy paper, maybe this means that he or she is rich," Alec said.

"Right," said Gina.

Alec wrote that down.

"Now this is the tough part. The person thinks whatever is stolen is rightfully his — or hers," Gina said. "Why would the person think that?"

Alec rubbed some more thoughts into his brain. While he was doing that, he looked around his room for some inspiration. His eyes landed on his train set.

"A will!" he said. "What if the person thought the missing whatever was supposed to be left to him — or her — in a will?"

"Oooh, that's really good," Gina said. "Write that down."

Alec wrote.

"What else?" he said, when he was finished.

"Well, there's what your dad told you about the cans and cans of blue paint. The person might have lots of blue paint, if those cans are a real clue and not a red herring. You know, a fake clue."

"I know what a red herring is," said Alec.

He wrote down the non-fake clue too. Then he did some more writing on a new page.

"Okay, here's the list," he said.

1) Probably rich (owns computer, fancy paper, no ransom money)
2) Probably wears cookie-smelling perfume or cologne
3) Probably has lots of blue paint and also maybe blue markers
4) Maybe thought missing something was left in a will

Alec's peanut butter brain was starting to churn at a much-faster-than-peanut-butter rate.

"What did Mrs. LaViolet say to you about her paintings?" he asked Gina.

"That they were monochromatic — and then she was impressed I knew that meant all one color."

"And what color were they?" Alec asked. He thought he knew, but he wanted to be sure.

"Blue," Gina said. "Oh my gosh, blue! Like the tons and tons of paint cans! Like the smudge on the note! You think she could be the thief? But she was so nice!"

"Well," said Alec. "She smelled like cookies when she walked in the room, and she's rich . . . but what would she think someone was going to leave her in a will?"

"Jackson Pollock!" Gina said, bouncing up off the floor. "I bet it has something to do with Jackson Pollock!"

"But, Gina, the Jackson Pollock painting that the town owns is still right where it's supposed to be, in the library — we saw it today."

"Oh," said Gina. "Right . . . Well, is there another one?"

"I don't think so," said Alec.

"Do you think the book you took out of the library about Jackson Pollock will tell you?"

"I don't know," Alec said.

He went over to his backpack and grabbed the book. He flipped through the pages, looking for a list of where all of Jackson Pollock's artwork was hanging or something. He didn't find any lists, but a title caught his eye: *Full Fathom Five*. Alec stopped his page flipping. He stared at the little image of *Full Fathom Five* for a long time. Then he looked at the description at the bottom of the page that said the painting was owned by the Laurel Hollows Public Library and was willed to them by Jackson Pollock. Alec looked at the words on the page next to the picture and read quickly. It said that Lee Krasner and Jackson Pollock had visited Laurel Hollows and spent a rainy afternoon in the library, reading through old diaries from the first settlers of Laurel Hollows. The couple had enjoyed their visit so much that Jackson Pollock had left the painting to the library in his will when he died.

"Gina!" Alec said, looking at the painting again. "Gina! Get over here!"

"What?!" Gina said, racing to him.

"This isn't the painting that we saw today in the library, is it?"

Gina looked. Then she gasped.

"No!" she said. "That's not it at all! The one we saw had legs and the scratchy eyeball in the corner. This one is all drips."

"Drips with a ghosted key," Alec said, pointing to a spot on the page. "Layers and layers and layers of drips."

"Wait, but didn't we see the one with the legs and eyeball in Ms. Blume's book?" Gina asked.

Alec was furiously rubbing thoughts into his brain.

"You're right!" he said. "We saw the legs, but it was in the other book! The Lee Krasner book!"

Gina's face looked like thoughts were racing into her brain too.

"And didn't Mrs. LaViolet say that she had some of Lee Krasner's most famous paintings in her collection?" she asked.

"And Ms. Blume said that the legs one was one of Lee Krasner's most famous!"

"Oh my gosh," Gina said. "Mrs. LaViolet is the thief! She has to be. She must've gone in while the library was closed or something and switched the paintings, and then since the librarians were out, no one knew!"

"Do you think it was just good timing?" Alec asked, the thought just occurring to him. "Or do you think she got the librarians sick?!"

"Oh, I hope it was good timing," Gina said. "Besides, Mrs. LaViolet couldn't make Mrs. Allen have babies."

"Good point," said Alec.

They were both quiet for a minute.

"But wait," said Gina. "We know what the missing something is and we know who took it, but we still don't know where it went."

Alec's peanut butter brain was working overtime. Now it was more like a . . . a . . . sports car brain, moving super fast.

"Oh yes, we do," he said. "Follow me."

And he ran downstairs with Gina hot on his heels.

12

Even Though He Hated Hamsters

Dad! Dad!" Alec yelled as he took the steps two at a time. "Dad, you have to take us over to the art show! Right now! We know who the thief is and we know what was stolen, and I think I know where it is!"

"What what what?!" Officer Flint said. "What are you saying?"

"It's Mrs. LaViolet and she stole a Jackson Pollock painting from the library, and I think it's hanging in the art show!"

"The woman who gave the public schools all that

money to teach about Jackson Pollock? You think she's the thief?"

"No, Dad," Alec said. "Not think. I pretty much *know* she's the thief."

"For real, Officer Flint," Gina said. "We did sleuthing and have all our facts and everything."

Officer Flint paused for a few seconds and then grabbed his jacket from the chair next to him.

"Okay," he said. "Let's go. You tell me your clues on the way, and if I agree, I'll call the department. This is a bit earlier than we planned on setting the trap, but I bet we can improvise."

So Alec, Gina, and Officer Flint jumped into the unmarked vehicle and drove to Laurel Hollows East while Alec and Gina explained the case and how they figured it out. Even before they got to the school, Officer Flint was convinced that the mystery had been solved and made a phone call to the police chief.

"Backup's on its way," he said. "Our job is to find the painting and the thief and make sure that neither of them goes anywhere."

He parked the car and pulled the key out of the ignition.

"Deal?" he said, sticking his hand out to both fourth graders.

"Deal," Alec and Gina repeated, shaking Officer Flint's hand at the same time — Alec shaking the thumb part and Gina shaking the pinky part.

"So, we've got to be calm about it — don't say anything that will make her want to run."

"Got it," Alec said.

Gina nodded.

The three of them walked into the building to the auditorium.

"Al," Officer Flint whispered. "We're early for the show, so this is our cover: You were excited to show me your painting, so we came to see if everything was set up already. You introduce me to this Mrs. LaViolet. Okay?"

"Sure," Alec whispered back, very excited that he was part of a cover. He'd never done that before. This was very good sleuth practice for when he got older.

"What's my job?" whispered Gina.

"Your job," said Officer Flint, "is to find the real *Full Fathom Five* and stand next to it."

"That should be easy," Alec told her. "It's the one that doesn't have a kid's name on the easel."

"Got it," said Gina. In the car he had explained all about the painting with the layers and layers of splatters that he saw Ms. Blume unwrapping right after school and how she was going to display it. He was certain that was the real Jackson Pollock, secretly hiding among paintings that looked a lot like it. Just like Gina and the *Little Women* book in the library. Just like the orange in the fruit bowl.

The show was all set up when they walked into the auditorium — and there were streamers and little cheese cubes and vegetables and crackers set out too. And also a plate of cupcakes with white frosting and colored frosting splatters on top. Alec couldn't wait to eat one. But sleuthing first, cupcakes second.

Following the plan for the cover story, Alec tugged on his dad's hand and dragged him over to the easel that said *Alec Flint* on it. Only when he looked up, he got very confused. His painting with the big button wasn't there. It was someone else's painting instead!

"Gina!" he called.

But Gina was already running over.

"Alec!" she said. "The painting on my easel isn't my painting!"

"And the one on mine isn't my painting either!"

The two super sleuths looked all around them at

the paintings filled with splatters and drips and flings. All in the wrong places.

"Do you think we can find the real one?" Alec whispered to Gina. "I remember it had a lot of paint on it."

"Alec, tons of these paintings have a lot of paint of them."

"What's going on?" Officer Flint asked, when he noticed all the whispering going on below him. "What happened to our plan?"

"Someone mixed up all the paintings, sir," said Gina. "We can't do the plan anymore."

"Well," said Officer Flint, "this proves to me that you guys are definitely on the right track. Let's forget about the real painting for now and find that LaViolet woman."

Gina scanned the room and saw silver hair in one of the corners. The person attached to it was wearing a flowing dress and a shawl and was straightening a painting on an easel. The plaque on the easel was different than Ms. Blume's handwritten ones — it looked like it was computer-printed on the same fancy paper as the note, but it was too far away to see what it said.

"She's over there," Gina said, pointing.

"Okay," said Officer Flint. "You kids introduce me. Come on."

The three of them trooped over to Mrs. LaViolet. She turned toward them, blocking the easel and the plaque behind her.

"Well, hello, darlings," she said, looking down toward Alec and Gina. "And who is this lovely man you've brought? Does he belong to one of you?"

"Um," said Alec. "He's my dad. Off — I mean, Edward Flint. Dad, this is Mrs. LaViolet. She's related to Jackson Pollock and gave us all the stuff to do this art show."

"Nice to meet you, Mrs. LaViolet," Officer Flint said.

"You too, dear," said Mrs. LaViolet. "You know, the show doesn't start for another couple of hours. I'm expecting some people before then, so you might want to take the children on a little walk. Besides, I wouldn't want you to see something that would ruin the big surprise."

"Oh! No, we wouldn't want to ruin any surprises," said Officer Flint. "I'm sorry we're early. It's just that Alec was so excited to show me his painting. . . ."

"That's right," said Alec. "How about I show it to my dad, and then we take a walk? I promise we'll be really quiet if your friends come. And we'll plug our ears if you have to talk about the surprise."

Alec's sports car brain was racing — what sort of surprise? Was she going to paint the art show blue? Was that the plan?!

Mrs. LaViolet's face got red and her hands clenched into fists. "Didn't anyone ever tell you not to challenge your elders, young man? Out! Out with all of you. The show starts in two hours!"

Alec took a step back. Gina took a step closer to him. And Officer Flint put his arms around both children.

"Mrs. LaViolet," Officer Flint said, "is there really harm in Alec showing me his painting before we go? He didn't mean any disrespect."

Alec shook his head. He didn't mean any disrespect at all. Especially not to a possible perp.

"Sir, I really would appreciate it if you left," said Mrs. LaViolet, a little bit calmer now. "Ms. Blume has gone to get apple juice, and I know she'd want to be here to tell you about the children's projects. And I really am expecting an important visit. So, please . . ."

Officer Flint nodded.

"Of course, ma'am," he said.

He started ushering Alec and Gina toward the

door. On their way there, Alec saw Pete Sanchez standing in the doorway. Officer Flint nodded one slow nod at him. Officer Sanchez nodded back. Then four police officers, dressed in their uniforms, marched into the auditorium.

"Penelope LaViolet, you're under arrest," Officer Sanchez said, "for the theft of public property. You have the right to remain silent. Anything you say can and will be used against you in a court of law."

"Get your hands off me! You have no proof!"

"But we will soon," said Officer Flint, standing next to his partner. "We know that you stole the Jackson Pollock painting *Full Fathom Five* from the Laurel Hollows Public Library, and we know that it's here at the art show."

"But . . . but . . . how did you know?"

"She just admitted it!" whispered Gina. "We're right!"

"Big-time," Alec whispered back.

"These children figured it out," Officer Flint said, indicating Alec and Gina.

And while Penelope LaViolet's attention was focused on the fourth graders, Officer Sanchez slipped handcuffs around her wrists.

"You forgot my threat," she said very quietly. "Everything will be blue by morning, unless you sign over that painting and let me go free!"

"Sorry, lady," said Officer Sanchez. "We found your stock of paints, and we found the guy you hired to do the vandalism while he was dropping off some more cans. No blue town for you. No painting either."

"You don't understand!" Penelope LaViolet yelled. "I love that painting. It was supposed to be mine! Jackson told me he'd leave it to me in his will. He promised! And then he willed the painting to this horrid little town. How could he do that to me? I asked to buy the painting back, but your stupid, prissy librarian wouldn't sell it. Not even when I tried to bribe her."

Mrs. LaViolet was breathing hard, and her cheeks were getting redder and redder.

"This town doesn't deserve that painting. You have one of the greatest artistic works of all time, and you display it in the basement of a library?! What's wrong with you?! It should be in a museum, with proper lighting and a security system. It should be the centerpiece of a collection! I *had* to steal it. It took me years of waiting to find the perfect time, to make the perfect plan! How could these children have figured me out?!"

"Well," said Officer Flint, "I think your donation to the school's art education program really helped. You paid for the method of your own demise. Now, you can make this easier on yourself if you tell us which painting is the stolen one. We can return it to the library and give you some leniency."

Mrs. LaViolet sighed.

"Are you sure the town won't sign it over?" she said. "Or let me buy it? I'm prepared to pay. And I would be happy to let other people see it, you know. That was my plan all along — to share Jackson's work with all the world. To show that painting as it was meant to be shown. Look, I even made a small easel to display it here, before finding a proper place for it. I'll need my Krasner back, of course — though there are some other paintings in my collection I'd be happy to loan your library — and then I'll display them together, as they should be shown."

She stepped sideways, pulling Officer Sanchez along, and revealed the wording on the plaque behind her. It said: *Jackson Pollock, The World's Greatest Abstract Expressionist.*

"See?" she said. "After Laurel Hollows signed the painting over to me, I was going to make it part of the art show. Demonstrate to the town that I meant them no ill will. I was going to share the painting with everybody. I just needed to get my hands on it first, to show you all how wonderful it looks when displayed properly. With proper lighting. Not in some godforsaken basement. It was all I could think to do, when your librarian told me that no amount of money would compel her to sell Jackson's painting. I still will pay, you know, if that makes things easier."

"Mrs. LaViolet," Officer Flint said, "that's a lovely sentiment, but the fact still remains that you stole a valuable painting from the library and it needs to be returned, regardless of whether you loaned another painting in its place or not, and regardless of whether you're willing to pay or not. I ask you again, which painting is the real Jackson Pollock? I'm assuming, from what the kids and I saw earlier, it's not the one currently on that easel."

"No, it's not," Mrs. LaViolet said. "This mix-up is my insurance policy. If you agree not to arrest me, I'll tell you which one is *Full Fathom Five*. I'm pretty certain no one in this town will be able to tell a real Jackson Pollock from the pieces the children created. The art teacher didn't even know. And no one realized when I swapped the Pollock for the Krasner either, which is really quite an abomination. An entire town that couldn't tell a Pollock from a Krasner!"

"Mrs. —" Officer Flint started to say, but Alec tugged on his pants.

"Don't worry, Dad," he said. "You don't have to offer her a deal. She's wrong. Gina and I can figure it out. I know we can. We figured out about the painting replacement, and we can figure out about this too."

Officer Flint was quiet for a minute.

"All right," he said. "Go for it."

Then he turned to one of the policemen who'd come in with Officer Sanchez.

"And you," he said. "Go to the school library or to the art room or wherever you can find a book of Jackson Pollock paintings. We're going to need proof positive."

Alec and Gina ran from painting to painting.

"Okay," Alec said, "we need one with lots of paint on it, because that's what I saw when Ms. Blume opened the package."

"What about this one?" Gina stopped in front of the easel with Mala Sharma's name on it. "There's a lot of paint."

Alec looked. There was a lot of paint. There were also a lot of ghosted buttons under the paint.

"The key!" he yelled. "We need to find the ghosted key! None of our paintings have one, but Jackson Pollock's does."

Alec and Gina looked, but couldn't find any keys in the painting on Mala's easel. Alec glanced over his shoulder at Mrs. LaViolet, who was looking very smug.

"I don't think it's this one," he whispered to Gina.

The two sleuths-in-training scanned the room.

"There," said Gina. "That one has a lot of paint too!"

They both ran over. It was Roy Michaels's easel. Gina found a ghosted button. Then Alec found a ghosted twig. And then at the same time they both yelled, "A key!"

They'd found the painting.

"Dad!" Alec cried. "Here it is!"

"Noooo!" wailed Penelope LaViolet. "I'm ruined!"

"Looks like you got it right, kids. Stay right there. We'll double-check when Officer Marx comes back."

Just then Ms. Blume came running in with three Jackson Pollock books under her arm. She was still wearing her jacket, and Officer Marx was jogging behind her, carrying two big bags filled with apple juice cartons.

"What happened?" Ms. Blume said, looking around. "This officer said you needed my books . . .

but . . . wait . . . all the paintings are in the wrong places!"

Officer Flint quickly explained what was going on, and Ms. Blume gave him the book with the *Full Fathom Five* image in it. He compared it to the painting Alec and Gina were standing in front of. It was the Pollock all right. The sleuths-in-training had done it again.

"I can't believe I didn't notice!" said Ms. Blume. "I had my hands on a real Jackson Pollock and didn't even realize it."

"It's okay," said Alec. "You like his earlier work better."

Ms. Blume smiled. "Exactly right, Alec," she said. "I really just can't understand any of this, though. A stolen painting . . . Mrs. LaViolet. I had no idea."

"That's because you, dear girl, are far too trusting," Mrs. LaViolet said loudly from the doorway where Officer Sanchez was leading her out. "Though you clearly taught these children quite well. I do appreciate the fact that my money was well spent, at least."

Then the policemen pulled her out of the auditorium and slammed the door behind her.

"Nice job, you two," Officer Flint said to Alec and Gina. "I think big congratulations are in order. And a cash reward too, if I remember the mayor's note correctly."

Alec and Gina beamed. Though Alec was feeling a little bit sad inside. He suspected Gina was too. Mrs. LaViolet seemed like she was mainly a nice person. Just a little bit . . . well . . . nuts to think she could steal a painting and get away with it.

"Listen, I have to get *Full Fathom Five* out of here," Officer Flint said, "and you two should help your teacher get the art show ready."

For the next hour or so, Alec, Gina, and Ms. Blume rearranged paintings, looking on the back for people's names and then putting them on the right easels. They finished just as the first students and their parents came walking into the show. One of the policemen had stayed to assure everyone that the thief had been arrested, and everyone looked happy. They were eating cupcakes, examining art, and chatting about the paintings.

Everyone, that is, except for Alec Flint. Even though he and Gina had just solved their second case, and were probably going to get a lot of money for it besides, Alec had no one to show his painting to. His dad was back at the police station dealing with *Full Fathom Five,* and his mom hadn't arrived. And probably wouldn't.

Alec sat down glumly on the floor, not even taking a cupcake with him. Gina's mom came over to him and said that after the show she'd love to interview him for the paper. Alec said sure, because being in the paper was very cool — especially if they put in another picture of him and Gina — but it didn't cheer him up all that much.

Then he heard someone calling his name.

"Alec?" the voice said.

Alec looked up. It was his mom! She was pulling a suitcase behind her and walking as quickly as she could.

"Mom!" Alec said, bouncing up off the floor. "You made it! You wouldn't believe what happened while you were gone!"

Mrs. Flint dropped her suitcase handle and gave Alec a hug.

"I spoke to your dad," she said. "He told me all about it! You and Gina did such a great job!"

Alec smiled as big as his lips would stretch.

"Yeah," he said, shrugging his shoulders. "You know, it wasn't that hard."

Mrs. Flint laughed. "I'm sure it wasn't," she said. "Not for brilliant super sleuths like the two of you."

The two Flints walked over to Alec's painting so he could tell his mom all about his big ghosted button. Then Gina came over with her family, and Emily came over with hers.

"I heard you and Gina solved the mystery," Emily said. "I didn't help this time."

Alec was about to tell her that she did — that she was the one who came up with the idea for the park, which is what made him think of the statues and other art the town owned. But before he could open his mouth, Gina opened hers.

"You totally helped, Emily," she said. "The park was your idea, and that led us to the ideas that solved the case. In fact, I bet Alec and I can share enough of our prize money that you can buy a hamster."

"Definitely," Alec said, even though he hated hamsters.

"Wow," said Emily. "You guys are the best — the best friends *and* the best sleuths."

Alec and Gina smiled at each other. They *were* the best sleuths, or at least the best sleuths-in-training. Now they'd just have to find their next case.

Alec Flint couldn't wait.

Author's Note

Even though this book about Alec Flint and his friends is fiction, Jackson Pollock was a real abstract expressionist who lived from 1912 until 1956. He married Lee Krasner, another abstract expressionist, in 1944, and the two of them moved from New York City, where they met, to a farmhouse on the east end of Long Island in a town called The Springs, where they lived until Jackson Pollock died. It was in their house there that Jackson Pollock first experimented with his famous drip painting technique, and there that he painted the work *Full Fathom Five,* which now resides in the Museum of Modern Art in New York City.

Laurel Hollows is, of course, a made-up town,

and the story of Jackson Pollock leaving a painting to the Laurel Hollows Public Library was something I created for this book. And Jackson Pollock did not have a cousin named Penelope LaViolet. She too is my own creation. However, all the paintings that I reference are paintings that Jackson Pollock and Lee Krasner actually did paint, and I've described what they look like as best I can. But being abstract paintings, the descriptions of the works are my own interpretations, and if you see these paintings someday, they may look completely different to you.

I did a lot of research, reading books and visiting museums, before I wrote this story. If you want to learn more about Jackson Pollock or Lee Krasner, I recommend reading the *Jackson Pollock* book in the Artists in Their Time series written by Clare Oliver. I also recommend visiting the Pollock-Krasner House — a beautiful museum created in the artists' former home on Long Island — and the many other places that exhibit Jackson Pollock's and Lee Krasner's art.

Jackson Pollock was a true leader in his field and one of the most influential artists in the twentieth century. I hope you enjoyed reading this story about his artwork as much as I enjoyed writing it.

— JILL SANTOPOLO
NEW YORK, NY

Code Translation

PAGE 4

Ms. Blume spoke on a purple cell phone in the school parking lot.

PAGES 109–110

Gina,

I don't have a note to come home with you. You have to get your mom to drive you to my house after the bus drops me off. We have to go over our clues for the case before the art show. It's our last chance to figure out what's stolen before the thief shows up.

   — Alec

Alec,

Okay. No problem. Your dad will be
there, right? We might need him.

— Gina

Yes.

Acknowledgments

Very special thanks go to Lisa Sandell, super editor; Jodi Reamer, super agent; Michael Stearns, super brainstormer; and David Gifaldi, super advisor. Thanks, too, to Marion Dane Bauer and Julie Larios's January 2007 Vermont College Workshop; all the folks at Scholastic who worked on Alec I and Alec II; and my family, friends, and teachers who inspired me to write these pages. It truly takes a village to raise a book, and I'm so thankful for every bit of help I received along the way.

About the Author

Jill Santopolo is not a super sleuth, but she is particularly good at identifying paintings — especially the ones displayed in museums in New York City, where she lives. She received a BA from Columbia University and an MFA from the Vermont College of Fine Arts. Jill's first book, An Alec Flint Mystery: *The* Niña, *the* Pinta, *and the Vanishing Treasure,* was also published by Orchard Books. When she's not writing her own books, Jill works as an editor, helping other books get published. You can visit her online at www.jillsantopolo.com.